# THE BRADYS' CHINESE CLEW

## CLEW

Francis Worcester Doughty

# CHAPTER I.
## CAUGHT IN A TRAP.

Late in the evening on August 12th, 19—, one of the heaviest thunder storms known in many years broke over the city of New York.

The storm was accompanied by a terrific gale; trees were blown down, sign boards wrecked, houses were unroofed, sewers overflooded, and there was a general shake-up all along the line.

Of course, lives were lost here and there, especially on the rivers.

It taxed the memory even of the oldest inhabitant to recall such another storm.

During the height of the gale two gentlemen sat in the famous Tuxedo restaurant, that delight of chop suey fiends and slumming parties, on Pell street, Chinatown, indulging in a late supper, Chinese style.

One was an elderly man of striking appearance and peculiar dress.

He wore a long blue coat with brass buttons, an old-fashioned stock and stand-up collar, while hanging to a peg above his head was a big white felt hat with an unusually broad brim.

His companion was a bright looking young fellow in his twenties.

The two men were none other than the world-famous detectives, the Bradys of the Brady Detective Bureau, Union Square, New York.

"Heavens, how it rains, governor," remarked Young King Brady as there was an extra loud splash against the window near which they sat.

"An awful storm, indeed," remarked the old detective. "It wouldn't surprise me if after all Mr. Butler did not come."

"He spoke in his letter of being quite feeble."

"Yes, and yet he gave his age at only sixty-five."

"Some men wear better than others."

"Decidedly so. We can only wait and see. I hate to disappoint Alice. There is no telling what difference it may make to her."

A deafening thunderclap interrupted the conversation.

Evidently the Bradys had come to Pell street for a purpose.

The storm continued to rage.

At twenty minutes past eleven the Bradys, who had held the table far beyond the limit by tipping their waiter, began to think it time to pull out.

"He will hardly come now," said the old detective. "Probably we shall hear from him to-morrow, but I am sorry we could not have finished up to-night. Alice is running a great risk, and I don't care to have her remain with that Chinese woman a moment longer than necessary."

He had scarcely spoken when a very young man, little more than a boy, in fact, entered the restaurant.

In his buttonhole he wore a yellow dahlia.

It was rather a singular flower for a boutonniere.

The Bradys noticed it at once.

"Look!" whispered Harry. "A yellow dahlia, the flower Mr. Butler was to wear so that we could identify him."

"Yes, but a young man—a mere boy. It must be a coincidence," the old detective replied.

"I don't know, governor. He has evidently spotted you. He is coming this way."

"Can Mr. Butler have sent a substitute?"

The boy approached the table.

He was dark and handsome, slightly undersized, and very well dressed.

"Excuse me," he said in a manly way, addressing the elder detective, "are you Old King Brady?"

"I am," was the reply.

"I thought so. My name is Butler—Ed Butler. My father had an appointment with you to-night at half-past ten; Mr. Edward Butler, of Albany. He was too sick to come to New York. He gave out at the last moment, so he sent me in his place."

"Sit down," replied Old King Brady. "You are terribly wet, my boy."

"Yes, it's raining like the dickens."

"Won't you have something to eat? A cup of coffee. You get good coffee here."

The boy sat down with a shudder.

"I don't want to eat anything in this place," he replied. "I think that mere knowledge that the food was prepared by a Chinaman would make it choke me."

"You don't like the Chinese, evidently," said Harry.

"Can you wonder? They have stolen my sister. Isn't that enough?"

"It is sad," observed Old King Brady, "but if white men will permit their daughters to act as teachers for Chinamen, what can they expect."

"That's what I say. I was opposed to Ethel having anything to do with that mission from the first, so was father, but mother encouraged her, and Ethel always would have her way. Now she has run off with a Chink, and I suppose it is the last we shall ever see of her. The minister who married them ought to be shot."

It was the old story.

Ed Butler's brief speech tells it. We need not enlarge.

Here was a pretty Albany girl, a mission worker, eloping with one of her Chinese pupils, a man years older than herself, and now her deluded mother sought to get her back again.

The Bradys would hardly have touched the case if it had not been that Mr. Butler occupied a government position at Albany, and they had been particularly requested by the chief of the Secret Service Bureau at Washington to take the matter up.

So far it had been only a matter of correspondence.

Old King Brady knew some things about the business which young Ed Butler did not know, and he was destined to learn still other things from a letter which the boy now delivered.

"When father found he couldn't come he wrote this, Mr. Brady," he said. "My orders were to deliver it to you before we made any talk."

"Ah!" said the old detective. "We will read the letter."

He did so.

It was quite lengthy.

Harry noticed that the old detective read certain parts of it over twice.

Folding it up and putting it in his pocket, at last the old detective turned to Ed.

"Are you much attached to Miss Ethel, my boy?" he asked.

"Why, sure—she's my sister," he replied quickly.

"I want the truth," said Old King Brady. "Certain points in your father's letter require me to ask the question. Be frank and honest now. You were constantly quarreling, were you not?"

"Sometimes we quarreled—yes. Ethel was rather hard on me."

"In other words, if she were not your sister you would not be in the least attached to her?"

Ed nodded, looking surprised.

"Well, I will say then for your benefit that the girl is no relation whatever to you. Your mother, as you are aware, is your father's second wife. You have always supposed Ethel to be your half sister, but she isn't even that. She is the daughter of Mr. Rawson, your mother's first husband by a previous marriage."

"Gee! I'm glad!" blurted the boy. "Now I can say what I really think. She's just horrid! I shouldn't shed a tear if we never found her, and that's a fact."

"So there is one load off your mind," observed the old detective.

"Yes, but why didn't my father tell me?" demanded Ed.

"He had sworn to your mother never to tell you. He instructs me to tell you, so that, in a way, he may not break his word."

"Poor pop," sighed Ed. "He certainly has a hard time of it. But what about Ethel? Is she here in Chinatown, as you supposed?"

"I believe such to be the case. My partner, Miss Montgomery, who has been working for three days on the matter, is to report to us to-night. Disguised as a Chinese woman, she

2

has been in a certain place where she expected to get information, and I have no doubt has done so by this time. We shall soon see her, and then you will know."

"Am I to go along?"

"Yes, by your father's particular request. He says this is the first time you have been to New York. He wants you to learn something of the city and its peculiar ways."

"All right. I have seen enough of it already to make me think that I never want to see it again."

"You decide hastily. If you have come directly from the Grand Central station, as I suppose——"

"That's right."

"Then you have seen very little of it, and that little under unfavorable circumstances. Wait for a daylight view of New York before you decide."

"Where do we go?"

"To a Chinese house around the corner on Mott street."

"I don't see how your partner can work in with the Chinks. Of course, she can't speak Chinese?"

"As it happens she can, and that is just where her advantage comes in. But come, let us go."

They passed out into Pell street.

The rain had now almost ceased, and the wind had died away entirely, but the gutters were running rivers.

"A tremendous amount of water must have fallen," Harry observed.

"Indeed yes," replied Old King Brady. "It has been a terrible storm."

He and Harry walked ahead. Ed walked behind, as there was not room enough on the narrow sidewalk for them to walk three abreast.

"There is more to this case than appears on the surface," Old King Brady whispered to his partner.

"It seems that this wretched girl has robbed Mr. Butler of three thousand dollars in cash, and also of a bunch of valuable papers. He does not want to get her back. His engaging us with that idea is merely a bluff for the benefit of the wife. He does want the papers, however, and if she will give them up he is willing that she shall keep the cash. I am sorry the man did not come himself. There seems to be some mystery about the papers which I fail to understand."

"He makes no explanation of their contents?"

"Nothing further than to say that their loss will probably involve him in a large loss of money. I don't just see what he can mean, for, as I understand it, Mr. Butler is merely working on a salary, and not a very heavy one at that."

"I should like to see the letter. Perhaps I can make something more out of it."

"Possibly, possibly, still I doubt it. I will show it to you first chance I get, and—— Good heavens! What was that?"

They had almost reached the point where Mott street joins with Pell.

Suddenly a crash had sounded behind them, and with it came a cry in a boyish voice:

"Help! Mr. Brady! Oh, help!"

Knowing, of course, that it could be no one else than the boy, Ed Butler, the Bradys instantly turned.

The boy had vanished.

Chinamen were running across the street, others were hurrying forward on the same side of the way.

There in the sidewalk was a large, gaping hole.

Two of the flagstones, undermined by the storm, probably, had sunk down just as the Bradys stepped off them.

Ed, less fortunate, had been caught in the break.

"Bless my soul! This is a great piece of business," cried Old King Brady.

Harry peered down into the hole.

It seemed to be pretty deep and it was also very dark.

Young King Brady could see nothing of the boy.

3

"Hello down there, Ed! Are you hurt?" he called.

"No; I'm all right. I went down with the stone. I'm not hurt a bit," came the answer, "but for heaven's sake get me out of here!"

It was easier said than done. The chattering bunch of Chinks crowding around offered no help.

"I don't see how in thunder we are going to get the boy up without a ladder," muttered Old King Brady.

"And where will we find one?" echoed Harry.

"That's the point. But here comes a policeman. Perhaps he can suggest——"

Thus far in his speech Old King Brady got when there came another call for help.

He could not exactly make out the words, but it was certainly, also, a cry of fear.

"Let go! Don't you touch me!" they heard now.

The cry came from the hole.

Then all was still below, although above the Chinamen chattered louder than ever.

"By Jove! the Chinks are going for the boy," cried Harry. "He has fallen into one of the secret dens of Pell street, sure!"

It looked like it.

The policeman came.

The Bradys turned electric flash lights into the hole.

It seemed to be a brick vault of considerable size.

But there was no one in it so far as they could discover.

Harry's repeated shouts to Ed brought no response.

"I must go down there and look for the boy!" cried Harry.

"Hold on," said the policeman, who was a person they knew; "if the Chinks have got him, they may get you, too. You know what Chinatown is."

"I ought to by this time!" cried Harry. "Lower me down, governor."

"The officer is right," said Old King Brady. "We better be sure than sorry. If we only had a rope."

"Look here, some of youse guys, get a rope!" cried the policeman, charging in among the crowd.

There were enough that understood him.

Some of them started to act.

A moment later a man came out of a Chinese grocery near by with a rope.

It was tied under Harry's arms and he was lowered into the hole.

The floor of the vault had water an inch deep upon it; the brick sides were dripping with a slimy ooze.

But there was no sign of Ed.

Nor was there any apparent opening except at the top.

The walls on all sides looked to be solid.

And Young King Brady saw now that they were up against another Chinese mystery.

But a mystery had also been revealed.

For the great storm had laid open one of the secrets of Pell street.

And who could say into what sort of a queer den this opening might lead?

## CHAPTER II.
### ED FINDS ETHEL.

Ed Cullen was not yet eighteen, although he looked to be twenty.

The boy, in fact, had but just graduated from the Albany High School.

He little dreamed into what peculiar adventures this visit to New York was destined to lead him.

The fall of the two flagstones came altogether as a surprise to Ed.

Doubtless the weight of the Bradys as they trod upon them completed the work of the water.

At all events, Ed had no more than planted his feet upon them when down they went.

The shock sent the boy on his knees.

He scrambled up and answered the Bradys as told.

Then an instant later Ed was seized from behind by two pairs of hands.

A secret door—bricks set in a box—had opened.

The boy, in spite of his struggles, was dragged through the opening.

Two Chinamen had captured Ed.

But why?

There was the mystery!

And we may as well add right here that just how it came about was never fully explained.

The chances are that the pair were inside the secret door when Ed fell, and hearing the noise, looked in upon him, although he did not see them.

A third Chink in American dress, which was not the case with the others, stood in a narrow passage holding a lantern.

Instantly Ed recognized him as Pow Chow, the Chinese mission worker who had run away with Ethel Rawson and caused all the trouble.

"You scoundrel!" cried Ed, who was nothing if not plucky.

He made a dive at the fellow and dealt him a stinging blow in the face.

It was a piece of folly, of course.

That was the time Ed got it good and plenty.

Pow Chow hit him over the head with the lantern.

The two others set upon the boy and gave him a good pounding.

Then having completely subdued him, for Ed saw that he was not in it, they dragged him along the passage through a door, and into one of the secret dens of Pell street, of which there are many, if rumor tells the truth.

It was a square room furnished in Chinese style and lighted by a hanging lamp.

The Chinaman gave Ed a shove and laughed when he landed on his back in a corner.

But Pow Chow did not laugh.

He came forward threateningly.

"You little fool! Whatever brought you to New York?" he demanded. "Looking for Ethel, hey?"

Pow Chow's English was perfect, for he was San Francisco born and his mother was a white woman, so he had always claimed, although he did not look like a half breed.

Ed picked himself up and glared at this man, whom he hated and despised.

"Where's Ethel?" he demanded, feeling that he had to say something.

"Never you mind where she is. What brought you here? Came to find her and to bring her back, I suppose. Well, she won't go."

"I haven't a thing to say to you," retorted Ed. "You let me out of here or Old King Brady will be after you. I want you to understand I am with him."

It was an exceedingly foolish speech.

The two Chinks began to chatter in their own language.

"Do you mean to say your father has set Old King Brady on to me?" demanded Pow Chow.

"Yes, he has. I was with him and his partner when I fell down into that hole. They'll be right after me. You let me go!"

Instead of answering, the man said something to his companions.

Evidently he gave the order to have Ed carried still further into these secret dens.

They immediately set upon the boy and blindfolded him.

Ed was then dragged out of the room, hurried upstairs and downstairs, through passages, up more stairs, and then down a long flight.

Resistance was impossible. A Chinaman had him on either side.

At last the journey ending, the handkerchief was removed, and Ed found himself in a little box of a room where there was a mattress flung down on the floor.

"There!" exclaimed Pow Chow. "Now we have brought you to a place where your friends, the Bradys, will never find you, Eddie. See that bed—it's yours for to-night—better get on it and make yourself as comfortable as you can."

5

And having said this, Pow Chow withdrew. His companions followed him, and Ed found himself a prisoner behind an iron door, which no power he could have exerted would budge.

And in that secret den Ed Butler stopped all night.

Worse still for the boy's peace of mind, he remained in that hot, stuffy place all the next day.

No one came near him.

At the end of his imprisonment Ed found himself a very uncomfortable boy.

Ravenously hungry, choked with thirst, despairing of ever getting help, he was thoroughly alarmed for his own safety.

He had almost come to the conclusion that Pow Chow meant to let him starve to death there in the secret den.

But no!

Relief came at last.

It did not come with the appearance of Pow Chow, however.

The two Chinamen who had captured him now appeared.

Ed was taken out and again blindfolded, was led by many devious ways to a large, well furnished room, which seemed to be on an upper floor, for he could see roofs out of a window.

There were several Chinamen sitting around smoking.

None of them paid any attention to Ed.

The idea now seemed to be to give the boy a chance to repair damages.

He was shown a sink, where he washed his face and hands.

Meanwhile a big, coarse looking white woman was busy putting food on a table.

A fairly good meal was spread, and Ed was told to eat.

By this time, as may well be imagined, the boy's prejudices had been overcome, and he demolished the food in short order.

Twice he asked about Pow Chow, and once what they intended to do with him, but no attention whatever was paid to his questions.

The meal over, one of the Chinamen offered him a cigar.

Ed had learned to smoke.

The cigar looked good to him, and he lit it, thinking that if he made himself sociable good might come of it.

It was just the reverse.

The cigar was drugged beyond all question.

Ed did not discover this until he had smoked fully half of it.

Then his head began to buzz.

He put the cigar down and staggered to his feet.

The Chinks were all watching him curiously the moment he made a move.

Ed tried to speak, but the words sounded like gibberish even to his own ears.

The room was whirling now.

Ed thought he was whirling with it.

The next he knew he was staggering backward.

He tried to get his balance, but it was impossible.

Falling, he struck the back of his head a blow which knocked him out completely.

When at last the boy came to his senses the scene had changed.

Ed now found himself lying on the bottom of a wagon with a pillow under his head.

He felt miserably sick and nauseated, and his head ached horribly.

The wagon was rattling over rough pavements.

He could see that it was being driven by an Americanized Chinaman; another of the same sort sat with him on the seat.

Slowly the boy began to pull himself together and to take in his situation.

His next discovery was that instead of being in his own clothes he was dressed in Chinese costume.

"Where can they be taking me? Whatever do they mean to do with me?" Ed asked himself.

6

But these were questions to which he could find no answer, of course.

He ventured to speak at last.

One of the Chinamen then produced a revolver, and looking back, stuck the weapon in Ed's face.

"Lookee here, you boy!" he growled, "keepee belly still; be belly good now or me shootee you dead—see? Dlat light. Me killee you if you makee fluss—see?"

Ed would have been dumb indeed if he had not understood the danger of his position.

He resolved to go slow, and he lay still for the remainder of the drive, which seemed interminable.

But it came to an end at last.

As Ed lay he could form no idea where he was going; indeed, he could not have told much about it anyhow.

All he had to go by was the fact that for the last half hour they had been driving along a country road.

He felt sure that they must have passed beyond the city limits for that reason.

At last the wagon stopped and one of the Chinamen got out.

He was gone some minutes, and when he returned Pow Chow was with him.

The latter climbed up into the wagon and looked in on Ed.

"Well, Eddie, how do you feel?" he demanded in a tone which seemed to be intended to be friendly.

"I feel bad enough even to suit you, I guess," replied Ed. "What have you brought me away out here for? What do you intend to do with me?"

"I intend to take you to Ethel if you will go quietly," was the answer. "If you won't do that, I suppose I shall have to take you by force. Which shall it be?"

"Oh, I'll go," said Ed. "Got to, I suppose. Does Ethel stand for the way you have treated me?"

"Ethel is my wife," replied Pow Chow. "She stands for anything I stand for—see? Get out and behave yourself now, Eddy, and you will come to no harm. I am sorry they kept you so long without feeding you. That was a mistake."

Ed now allowed Pow Chow to help him out of the wagon.

The effects of the drugged cigar had not altogether departed yet, as he found when he got on his feet.

They were out in the country and close to the shore of some large body of salt water, but it was not the ocean. Ed could see lights on the opposite shore, which seemed to be a long distance away.

They turned up a lane and came to a small frame house standing back among trees. Ed could not see any other house near.

Pow Chow led him around to the rear, and as they approached Ed saw Ethel appear at the open door.

The foolish girl was flashily dressed in Chinese female costume, wearing a red silk blouse and yellow trousers with Chinese shoes on her feet.

There were imitation diamonds in her hair and a big one in the form of a brooch was at her throat—perhaps she thought them real.

She looked to Ed so ridiculous that he could hardly refrain from laughing.

But he controlled himself and she came out to meet him.

"Oh, Eddie!" she exclaimed. "So you've come. I could hardly believe dear Pow when he said he meant to fetch you. How did you leave them all at home? Of course, I don't care what Mr. Butler thinks, but is mother very mad with me?"

"Indeed she is! I left her sick in bed," replied Ed. "Oh, Ethel, how could you ever be such a fool?"

"Come, shut up. None of that talk," said Pow Chow gruffly. "Go on in."

They entered, Ethel leading the way to a little parlor.

"We have taken this house, furnished, for a few weeks," she said. "You see we had to hide, for, of course, I knew father—I mean Mr. Butler—would send detectives after us. I hear he did it, too—the Bradys. You were with them last night. Tell me all about it, Eddie, and then perhaps I'll tell you something which will make you open your eyes."

"Come, cut that out!" broke in Pow Chow. "We haven't decided yet whether to tell him or not, you know. Anyway, we have got him safely out of Chinatown. I understand the Bradys were looking for him half the night."

"And they didn't find him. Oh, I am so glad. It's a shame he had to suffer so, though. I think you might have made it easier for my brother, Pow."

Ed was on the point of breaking in with: "I'm not your brother," but he concluded that it would pay him best to hold his tongue until he understood better what all this meant.

He had his suspicions, however.

He felt quite certain that it had something to do with the papers stolen from his father about which there had been much mystery.

Ed knew something about these papers, but not all.

What he knew we shall later explain.

## CHAPTER III.
### WORKING FOR A CHINESE CLEW.

It was true that the Bradys spent much time searching for Ed.

In this they were aided by a wardman from the Elizabeth street station, who was supposed to know much about the secret dens of Pell street, and we want it understood that the Bradys are by no means ignorant on that subject themselves.

But as it happened they did not know of any secret dens under that particular house, nor did the wardman, nor could they find any. At last they broke down the wall on two sides of the vault from which Ed had vanished.

Then they discovered the secret passage.

They traced it to its end, and it took a turn, bringing them in under another house.

Here there were two secret rooms where there had once been a private joss house conducted by the Chinese "Tong" or guild known as the Brother of the Red Door.

This particular place, as it happened, had been pulled by the Bradys about a year before.

They found the rooms empty and deserted.

Thus they missed it so far as Ed was concerned, and they finally gave up, feeling satisfied that they had overlooked some hidden door or passage which, of course, must have been the case.

It was now too late to look up Alice, as intended.

Where she was must now be explained.

Alice some time before had made a friend of a certain Chinese woman whose husband was a sort of detective or spy for the On Leong tong or merchants society in Chinatown.

This man's operations were confined to his own people.

He also knew Alice and liked her.

It was he who suggested that she come to his wife's rooms in Chinese disguise, and so be on hand ready to talk with the missing girl as soon as he could locate her, which he felt quite certain he would be able to do, for he had received positive knowledge that the girl had been seen in Chinatown along with an Americanized Chink, a stranger there, whom he believed to be Pow Chow.

But it would have done the Bradys little good if they had taken Mr. Butler to Alice, as they originally intended to do, for the detective did not come home that night.

Next morning his wife heard that he had gone to Chicago on business for the On Leong tong, so Alice gave it up, and about nine o'clock turned up at the offices of the Brady Detective Bureau, on Union Square, in her ordinary dress.

"Oh, you are here," exclaimed Old King Brady. "Harry was just going down to Chinatown to look you up. I suppose you are wondering what became of us last night?" and he went on to explain.

"This is a bad beginning," remarked Alice. "I don't know that I can help any more, either," and she went on to tell about the Chinese detective being called away.

"I am sorry," said Old King Brady. "I should have liked to have had his advice. The disappearance of that boy is certainly a puzzle. I shall never rest until I have found him. I wish now I had never touched the case."

"It does look pretty hopeless," remarked Harry, who had entered just in time to overhear this remark, "but never mind. We will get there. One thing, though. If it was me I wouldn't do a thing further than to try to find the boy until I knew more about the case. Mr. Butler ought to at least tell us what these papers are he is so anxious to find."

"He is singularly reticent about them," replied Old King Brady, "frank as he is on other points, especially his dislike for his wife. But we must decide upon some course of action. I don't propose to be downed."

Just then a clerk handed in a card.

It was a lady's visiting card and bore the name of Mrs. Butler.

"Another surprise," muttered Old King Brady. "Not satisfied with sending his son to us, the man has now sent his wife."

The visitor proved to be an overdressed, loud-voiced woman of forty odd.

"I suppose you are surprised to see me, Mr. Brady!" she exclaimed, making eyes at the old detective as she proceeded to seat herself. "The fact is, Mr. Butler was taken sick. He sent his son to you yesterday. The foolishness of it. Ed is a good boy, but he is only a boy. Where is he? Has he been here yet?"

"No, madam, he has not been here," replied Old King Brady, who saw at once that the woman was acting on her own account, and probably without the knowledge of her husband.

"The lazy fellow has probably overslept himself," said the woman, working her fan. "Just like him. I thought it might be so. I am just as well pleased. I wanted a chance to talk to you first. Have you heard anything of Ethel—my daughter, I mean?"

"No, madam; nothing definite as yet," replied the old detective.

"I was afraid it would be so. Pow is a very slick fellow. But you must certainly find her, Mr. Brady. You see, not only do I love the poor deluded girl dearly, but she has robbed us. Three thousand in cash, Mr. Brady; money that I have been saving for years. Then there are certain important papers. Those are what we are most anxious to obtain."

"Yes, ma'am. And what may the nature of those papers be?" the old detective asked.

"That I should prefer not to explain."

"But, my dear madam, you leave us in the dark. How can we be expected to find papers of which we know nothing?"

"Oh, you just find my daughter. She will give up the papers quick enough."

"You are sure?"

"Quite sure if I can only once get my hands on her."

"Where are you staying?"

"I haven't made up my mind yet. You see I came here directly from the train. I shall make it a point to send you my address once I am located."

"And this boy! Shall we send him home?"

"That will be the best way, if he will mind you. He never will me. He is a wild, harum-scarum fellow. It was perfect nonsense to send him here to look for his sister. But I wish you would tell me what you have done. I understood from Mr. Butler that you had learned that Ethel was here along with her Chinese husband."

"We have learned that much, Mrs. Butler, but we have been unable to locate her."

"It is too bad. I suppose Mr. Butler considers it all my fault. I don't. Pow persuaded Ethel to act as she did, I am sure. I don't know as I am to be held accountable in such a case."

Old King Brady all this time had been sizing the woman up.

With her husband's letter in his pocket, which told him of family jars, accusing Mrs. Butler of aiding and abetting Ethel in her Chinese escapade, and even hinting at the necessity of a speedy divorce for the writer, he saw plainly that some powerful motive other than love for her adopted daughter must have influenced her when she made this sudden move.

9

He resolved to shake her off and turn her over to Alice, telling her nothing about Ed.

"Mrs. Butler," he said, "let me be perfectly frank with you. Since Mr. Butler could not come to us, we must decline to pursue this case any further. All I have been able to learn about your daughter came to me through a certain female detective, a woman who is partly Chinese. She has a room on Pell street, in Chinatown. Better see her this afternoon. I happen to know that she will be in her room at three o'clock. No doubt she will be glad to help you along in the matter. She is a person you can rely on."

The woman looked surprised.

Old King Brady felt that she also looked rather relieved.

"What is this woman's name?" she asked.

"Her real name is Chinese. I forget it," was the reply. "She goes by the name of Gertrude Brown. Here is her address."

Old King Brady scribbled name and address on a slip of paper and passed it over to Mrs. Butler.

"Are her charges high?" the woman asked.

"Just the reverse. She is very reasonable, while our charges are high. Tell her that I sent you and that I have dropped the case. She will use you right."

"I am sure I am very much obliged to you," said Mrs. Butler, rising to depart. "But about Ed. You will send him home if he comes to you?"

"Yes, if you so desire."

"I do."

"Don't you want to see him?"

"No. I want him to go home. Tell him to go at once."

"But in case he won't go and insists upon your address?"

"I will give it to Miss Brown. I shall be settled by the time I see her."

Old King Brady let her go then.

He immediately summoned Alice, who had retired to her own office before Mrs. Butler was shown in, and told her what he had done.

"You want to get down to the rooms and take this woman in charge," he said. "Pump her dry. We want to find out what she is driving at if we can. You are to make up as you did before, but not quite so much like a China woman."

At the time of which we write, the Bradys were holding two rooms under rental on the top floor of a building on Pell street.

It was almost a necessity, for they had a great many Chinese cases to handle.

Alice assented.

A little later Old King Brady and Harry went to Chinatown again, and with the aid of the wardman made a thorough search for Ed.

But it came to nothing.

The same ground was gone over again; other secret dens were visited on the block.

But it is always hard work in Chinatown without a clew.

When detectives visit the Chinese houses, no objections are ever offered to a search, nor is any help ever given.

The Chinese sit around perfectly indifferent, seemingly.

Once in a while bribes will do the business.

Old King Brady found even that resource hopeless on this occasion, however.

After a hard day's work he had to give it up.

"I am afraid they have done for that boy," he remarked to Harry. "It indeed looks like a hopeless case."

He felt very much distressed about it, feeling somewhat to blame.

His next move was to call up the Government office, at which Mr. Butler was employed, but word came over the wire that the man was home sick.

All Old King Brady could do was to write him a letter, stating the facts, which he did, in time for the evening mail.

At a quarter to three o'clock Harry turned up at the rooms on Pell street.

Alice admitted him.

"Has Mrs. Butler come yet?" he asked.

"Not yet," replied Alice.

"The governor has decided that I am to be a witness to your conversation."

"I am glad of it. I don't want to take the responsibility alone."

They sat talking until quarter past three, when Mrs. Butler appeared.

Harry slipped into the other room when her knock was heard.

Alice took the woman right in hand, but she learned nothing more than the Bradys already knew.

Mrs. Butler wanted to find her daughter, that was all.

She only hinted vaguely at stolen papers.

All attempts to draw her out on that subject were in vain.

All Alice could do was to ask her address, which she gave, and to tell her to call next day.

It was a certain street and number in Brooklyn.

As for Ed, she never mentioned his name.

"She's a bad one," observed Harry after she had gone. "I take no stock in that woman."

Alice took none either.

"I am going around to Mrs. Fang's to see if she has any word for me," she said, referring to the wife of the Chinese detective. "I'll see you at the office if there is anything to report."

But there was nothing, and that day closed, leaving the case involved in mystery.

Next day Old King Brady had Alice write a Chinese advertisement offering $200 reward for any information which would lead to the discovery of Ed Butler's whereabouts.

This Harry posted on the dead wall at the corner of Pell and Doyer streets, where hundreds of little red slips can be seen any day.

This wall is called the Chinese bulletin board, also the Chinese newspaper.

Old King Brady offered the reward on his own account, but the address given was Alice's, on Pell street, and a Chinese name was signed.

Knowing that if anything was to come of it, early evening would be the probable time. The Bradys were on hand at the room right after supper.

At about half-past seven o'clock there came a knock on the door.

Old King Brady and Harry slipped into the other room, leaving Alice to open the door.

An aged Chinaman stood outside.

Alice asked him his business in his own language.

The answer was rather a surprise, for it came in pigeon English:

"Me wantee see Kling Blady."

"Old King Brady is not here," replied Alice. "What makes you think that?"

"Oh, me know. He camee here. Me see. Me know you, too."

Seeing that the case was hopeless, Alice asked him inside.

The old fellow shuffled into the room and looked around cautiously.

"Come," said Alice, "tell me what you want."

"Bout boy?" was the reply. "No telle you. Only tellee Kling Blady."

The old detective walked into the room.

He did not know the man so far as he could remember.

Nor was he particularly surprised at the situation, for he had taken no steps to conceal his identity.

"Hello, John! Here I am. Now what you got to say to me about that boy?" he asked.

"Money," replied the Chink. "Me can tell. Two hlundled dlollar—yair."

"You are up against it, governor," laughed Harry. "Do you propose to pay in advance for your Chinese clew?"

Old King Brady's answer was a roll of bills.

"I should have looked out for the boy better," he said. "I am willing to pay for my carelessness."

"See, John," he added, holding up ten ten-dollar bills, which he spread out like a fan. "Half now; other half when we get the boy."

11

The old man eyed the bills longingly, but shook his head.

"No tellee," he said. "You givee two hlundled dollars, den me tell."

"Get out," said Old King Brady, pocketing the bills. "You're a fraud. You don't know anything about the boy."

## CHAPTER IV.
### SUNKEN TREASURE.

It was about ten o'clock in the evening when Ed Butler arrived at his sister's house.

The location we may as well state was up in the Bronx, beyond Port Morris docks—we do not care to be more definite.

It was back of a little strip of water front which as yet remained unimproved.

Entering the house after a few words with Mrs. Pow Chow, who seemed disposed to shield her husband from blame, charging that Ed "struck him first," and so on, the three found themselves seated in the kitchen.

Pow lit a cigarette, and, turning to his wife, asked:

"Well, Ethel, shall I tell Eddie what we want of him to-night?"

"You can do as you like," replied the girl, "but if it was me I wouldn't tell him a blessed thing. I'd just make him do it, that's all."

"Do what?" demanded Ed, whose temper was rising under the contemptuous way in which the girl seemed disposed to treat him. "You will find that it won't be so easy to make me do what I don't want to, I guess."

"Sure," said Pow. "Now don't be so soon, Ethel. Eddie's a good boy. He's a kind of brother of mine, too."

"Not on your life!" cried Ed. "Ethel is no sister of mine."

"I could slap your face for you, you sassy little brat!" cried the girl, springing up. "How dare you talk like that? I guess I have a right to marry who I like. I'm of age, anyhow."

"Sit down!" cried the Chinaman. "Sit down and hold your tongue."

Then they began scrapping, Ethel resenting this kind of talk.

Ed thought it a good chance to try to pull out.

While they were in the midst of it he jumped up and made a bolt for the door, but Pow Chow was too quick for him.

The Chinaman got him by the neck in the hall and dragged him back, jamming him down into a chair.

"Now, now, now, Eddie!" he cried. "Don't make it any harder for me than you have to. I want to be good to you, but this is the limit. Be good, and you won't regret it—that's right. Say, Ethel, there's no use in us quarreling. According to your own account you and Eddie never could pull together. Go on upstairs and leave him to me."

Somewhat to Ed's surprise the girl flounced out of the room without a word.

Pow Chow lit another cigarette and offered the package to Ed.

"No, I don't want to be drugged again," growled Ed.

"You need have no fear. I only made them give you that cigar to keep you quiet. It was just opium. A little of it hurts nobody. I want to be a friend to you, Ed. Now let me tell you that it was all a surprise to me when I found who it was those two fellows had captured last night, but when I saw you it occurred to me that you being such, a bully swimmer and diver, that you were just the fellow I wanted—see?"

Wily Pow Chow!

He had touched Ed on his weak point, interesting him at once.

For Ed had a record for swimming, and particularly for diving.

It was his hobby and his pride.

Of course, he at once began to wonder in what direction his talents in this line were to be displayed.

"Use me how?" he asked.

"You remember those papers?" pursued Pow Chow.

"What Ethel stole from my father?"

"Yes."

"I know they were papers father found when the carpenters were altering over our kitchen a few weeks ago, that's about all."

"Not all, Ed. You knew that Mr. Butler expected to make money out of them?"

"I heard him say so—yes."

"But you don't know how, nor what it was all about?"

"No."

"Nor am I going to tell you, for now that you have brought the Bradys in on the business, they being Secret Service men, it might get you into trouble."

"A lot you care about me."

"More than you think, perhaps. I will tell you this, they referred to money which has been hidden under water long ago. I know the place. It is close by here, Ed. Remember when your father went to New York after finding the papers?"

"Yes, I do."

"Well, he located the place then, or pretty near it, but not being a swimmer, he could do nothing, so he came home to think it over. He told your mother, and she told Ethel, and Ethel told me, but what none of us knew was just where this money was hidden; that the old man, wise guy that he is, kept to himself, but he wasn't wise enough not to write it down, and that's what he did. He put that paper along with the rest. Ethel got the whole bunch before she came away. I have them now."

"And the money you stole from my mother!" cried Ed bitterly.

"Yes," was the cool reply. "We thought we might as well make a clean sweep. But to get back to business. I don't know how to swim. As it happens, I don't know anyone who does. My people are not much given to swimming and diving, so when fortune threw you in my way I at once thought that I might as well use you. All in the family, you know. Will you be sensible and help? or will you be ugly and force me to make you trouble? I hired this house so as to be near the spot. I am prepared to act to-night. If you'll help me out, it's halves between us. What do you say?"

"How can I say anything when I know so little? How much money is there?"

"Sixty thousand dollars."

"And who does it belong to?"

"Uncle Sam!"

"The Government?"

"Yes."

"Who hid it?"

"Oh, well, since you insist upon knowing, it was hidden by a pension agent who used to live in that house of yours up at Albany years ago. He robbed the Government. His wife was sick and dying; that's what made him sneak back to Albany. She died. He must have gone crazy, for he wrote out an account of where he had hidden the money. This he hid in the house, and then shot himself. Your father, who works in the pension office, as you know, knew all about the business. It happened ten years ago. Five years ago he hired the same house. When he was clearing out things in the kitchen to get ready for the carpenters, he came across the papers. That's the whole story, Ed. He would have swiped the money himself if he had been able to get it. Now it's my turn."

"I don't believe it."

"Never mind whether you do or not. Will you help me get that money, Ed? That's the point."

Ed had been doing a lot of thinking.

If he refused he could see nothing ahead for himself but trouble.

There was nothing to hope from Ethel.

He believed Pow Chow bad enough to kill him, and he was not at all sure that Ethel would not urge him on.

On the other hand, he was sure the Chinaman could not swim, and he felt that if he could once get the money there was nothing to hinder him from swimming away with it.

The boy's reasoning, right or wrong, brought him around to the determination to make the attempt.

That Pow Chow had any intention of giving up one dollar in his clutches Ed did not for an instant believe.

"All right," he said. "I'll go you, Pow. I only hope you mean to play fair with me."

Pow assured him in the most solemn manner that he meant nothing else.

He seemed greatly pleased at Ed's ready assent.

Ethel was called and told.

She had recovered her good humor by this time and she made herself very agreeable.

A supper was spread and they all sat down to it.

Pow Chow was very curious to know how Mr. Butler ever came to take up with the Bradys.

Ed could not answer this, however.

He had been told nothing about the Bradys till his father, being taken sick, ordered him to go to New York and meet them.

Inwardly he was wondering what his father's real intentions were.

As for his mother, Ed knew her too well to imagine for a moment that Uncle Sam would ever have seen any of the stolen money if she could get her hands on it.

It is a sad thing for a boy to have no confidence in his mother, but such was Ed Butler's case.

Ed now asked to see the paper, which his father had drawn up, but the wily Chinaman refused to exhibit it.

"I've been over the ground. I'll point out the place. That will be all you need," he said.

"And when do we go?" asked Ed.

"We will make it midnight," replied Pow Chow.

"Hark!" whispered Ethel suddenly. "It seems to me that I hear someone outside the window."

Pow, with a muttered exclamation, started to rise.

"Sit down, clumsy," breathed Ethel. "Let me see."

She slipped out into the hall and opened the back door suddenly.

Instantly the sound of skurrying feet was heard.

"Pow! Eddie! Quick!" cried the girl.

They were right behind her, but too late to see any one.

There was no fence around the yard. Beyond was a vacant lot overgrown with bushes.

"Two Chinks!" cried Ethel. "I saw them dive in among the bushes there."

Pow was furious.

Drawing his revolver, he ran out, but Ethel called him back, and he came.

"You have been talking, sir!" she cried. "That's what it means. You have been shooting off your mouth to your Chinese friends about this business. That's what, and it is a shame now that we have got Eddie to help us, and everything is so nicely arranged!"

Pow swore he had not, but Ed did not believe him.

The Chinaman seemed very nervous after that, and he kept on the watch for some time, but nothing more was seen or heard of the intruders.

Midnight came at last.

After the alarm all conversation was held in whispers.

Ed suggested that they get on the job.

Ethel was for postponing everything, but Pow was for going ahead, and he had his way.

About half-past twelve, after a careful look around, Ed and the Chinaman started out.

Ethel wanted to go along, but her husband sat down upon it.

Pow ordered her to lock the doors and windows and keep close till their return.

He seemed very nervous as they walked on down a narrow lane which took them to the shore.

Here there was a stretch of rocks against which the water came.

Beyond was a ruinous pier, at the head of which was the foundation of a large building apparently destroyed by fire a long time before.

The neighborhood was lonely enough at all times, and now it appeared to be utterly deserted save for themselves.

"If it wasn't for that scare we had, I should feel sure that we were going straight to success," growled the Chinaman. "I only wish I could have seen those fellows for myself. I can't imagine who they could have been."

"Mebbe they were the same ones who brought me up here," suggested Ed.

Pow, however, did not think so.

They went down on the pier.

The tide was up and the night dark.

"Now then, what am I to do?" demanded Ed.

"It is like this," said Pow. "The paper written by the pension agent says that he put the money in a water-tight tin case, tied a heavy stone to it, and sunk it alongside the seventh pile from the end of the pier where the water is about fifteen feet deep at high tide. Is it that now, I wonder?"

Ed did not know.

Having been brought up in Albany, tides were a mystery to him.

"I can only try it," he said, "and I may as well go about it now."

He began to undress.

"Look about well when you get into the water," said Pow. "Those fellows might be hiding under the pier."

Ed assented.

Stripped in a minute, he stood looking down into the water.

"Why don't you go ahead? What are you hanging back for?" the Chinaman demanded.

"A fellow hates to dive where he doesn't know the depth, especially at night," replied Ed.

"Oh, go ahead! I only wish I could dive. I wouldn't hesitate."

"Well, here goes!" cried Ed, and throwing out his hands he dove off the pier.

## CHAPTER V.
### FOLLOWING UP THE CHINESE CLEW.

Old King Brady hardly knew how to handle the old Chinaman.

The man's face was as expressionless as a wooden block when he said:

"Me no talkee, boss. Two hlundled dlollars, den me tellee you sometling big. No givee me, go away."

"Something big?" queried Old King Brady. "You mean something more than just about the boy?"

"Yair, whole lot more. Me no dlead one. Some fellers tlink me dlead one—no."

What was he driving at?

Old King Brady's curiosity was fully aroused.

At last he ended it by counting out another hundred and placing the whole in the Chinaman's hand.

The old fellow chuckled.

"Now then, John, out with the whole business," said Old King Brady, "and let your name come along with the rest."

And the old detective found no reason to regret his bargain.

"Me talkee Chinee to lady now," said the old fellow.

"Right. Go ahead," assented Old King Brady.

The conversation was quite extended.

"Is it important, Alice?" Old King Brady ventured to ask while it was in progress, for it seemed as if they would never come to an end.

"Most important," replied Alice. "You better let me hear all he has to say."

At last she turned and began to translate.

"It seems," she said, "that this old fellow, whose name is Fen Wix, as near as I can make out, although I never heard the last name before, is supposed to be deaf. He is so at times, but there are times when his hearing is perfect. He says that they have taken the boy

15

away up into the Bronx to a cottage on Lorimer's lane, near the ruins of an old fertilizer factory; that is all the description I can get of the place."

"And it happens that I know it," replied Old King Brady. "There was once a fertilizer factory at the foot of Lorimer's lane. It burned some years ago."

"Pow Chow and his white wife are there in that cottage. They have a scheme to recover a lot of stolen money sunk in the water near by. Pow knows where. He was looking for a Chinaman who could swim and dive. He drank too much last night and talked about his plans to two men, both Chinese. This old fellow overheard, although they supposed he could not hear. He says that these two men are out for this treasure. The boy, it appears, is an extraordinary swimmer, and the plan is to use him. Fen Wix thinks that Pow Chow will have no recollection of the talk he made. He considers these two men his enemies, and yet he will not give away their names. He says that because he hates them and because he is too old to go after the treasure himself, he is giving the secret away to you, as he needs money. That is the gist of his story."

"Sounds rather fishy, don't you think so, governor?"

"Oh, I don't know," was the reply. "It seems to explain Mrs. Butler's anxiety and some other things. It may be that these mysterious papers give an account of the hiding of the treasure. I think there may be something in the thing."

"Dere sure is! Dere sure is, Boss Blady!" cried Fen Wix, who had been listening to all this. "You goee head. You win out. Me no can do nluffin, see? You gimmee two hlundled dlorrar, dat better as nluffin—see? Goee head. You win—see?"

And such was the Bradys' Chinese clew.

Chinamen rarely go out of their way to inform on each other, but sometimes they do. A desire for revenge is the usual motive.

Fen Wix told Alice that he was seventy-six years old, and that one of the men to whom Pow Chow blabbed the secret in his cups ought to support him, but instead had treated him shabbily.

He would not say whether the man was any relative to him, but Alice assumed that such was the case.

"Do you think Pow Chow means to set the boy diving for this treasure to-night?" Old King Brady asked.

"Me tlink yair," was the reply. "Me no can tellee, but me tlink yair. You go?"

"Yes, I'll go. How much money is there?"

"Me no know. Pow Chow no tellee dlat."

"Who was it stolen from?"

"Me no know dlat neder. Me no can tellee dlat. You go?"

"Yes, yes, I'll go," replied the old detective.

"Dlen you better go quick. So you win, lemember, old man, gimme more money—see?"

"Perhaps I will," assented the old detective. "We'll see what it all amounts to first."

And with that Fen Wix departed.

"A most peculiar piece of business," observed Harry. "I must say I am very much afraid you have blown in your money for nothing, governor."

"Don't croak," replied the old detective. "What's a couple of hundred, anyway? I shan't cry if it all proves romance, but how would that old Chink have the location down so pat unless there was something in what he says?"

This, of course, was the strongest argument which could be urged, and Harry raised no further objections.

One significant fact was that nobody else appeared to have been attracted by the reward, for no one came.

"We will start for the Bronx now," said Old King Brady. "Alice, my dear, it seems hardly worth while for you to join us. Will you stop here to-night or will you go home?"

"Neither," replied Alice. "With your kind permission I will go along."

"I supposed you would say so. Be quick then and do away with your disguise."

Alice retired and made her change.

It was shortly after nine o'clock when they started, and they were certainly due at their destination long before midnight, and would have reached it if Old King Brady had not blundered.

Nor is it any wonder.

Conditions in the Bronx have changed so of late, old landmarks disappearing so rapidly, that anyone relying on memory alone gets mixed up.

And this is precisely what Old King Brady did.

He found himself at fault almost at the start.

He could not locate Lorimer's lane.

Then they started to inquire their way.

This only made matters worse.

Nobody ever knows anything when one comes to inquire their way up in the Bronx about old-time roads and lanes.

At last an ancient individual was found who claimed to be able to direct them, and the Bradys came out on the water front where there was a lane, a ruined factory and an old pier.

It was now about eleven o'clock.

Old King Brady was sure that he had hit the right spot.

Harry and Alice knew nothing about it.

They began to look about for the cottage.

There were two on this lane, both still lighted up.

Harry ventured to peer in at the windows of each.

The report was unfavorable.

He saw no Chinaman inside.

Old King Brady then made some inquiries at a lonely saloon which stood on a corner, with lots on all sides.

The place was deserted save for a sleepy bartender.

He assured the old detective that such a thing as a Chinaman was unknown in the neighborhood.

They got inside the ruined factory and watched the pier until midnight, but not a soul came near the place.

Harry was triumphant.

"It's all a fake," he declared, "and you are out your two hundred. We may as well ring off and go home."

He had scarcely spoken when an old man with a fishing basket, a pole and a lantern came hobbling onto the pier.

"At last!" muttered Old King Brady. "Here is a party who, if he belongs in the neighborhood, may know something."

He stepped out into view.

"Good-evening, uncle!" he called.

"Evening yourself," growled the old man. "If you mean to hold me up you won't get nothin', I tell yer that straight. I hain't even begun to fish."

"I'm no hold-up man. On the contrary, I'm a detective."

"What say? I'm a bit deef. I can't hear."

"What building is this?"

"That? Why, that is Niebuhr's old moulding mill. It burned down five years ago."

"It isn't Fisher's fertilizer factory, then?"

"No, no! You're all off. That's a mile and over up the shore."

"But wasn't this lane behind us once known as Lorimer's lane?"

"So it was."

"I thought Fisher's fertilizer factory stood at the foot of Lorimer's lane?"

"So it did."

"Explain yourself."

"Well, the explanation is easy enough, boss; there's two Lorimer's lanes."

This settled it.

Bestowing a dollar on the lone fisherman in exchange for his information, Old King Brady started in to rectify his blunder.

They made the best time they could up the shore, but it was with little hope of accomplishing anything it had now grown so late.

Indeed, it was nearly one o'clock before they came in sight of another pier with the foundation of a burned building at the end.

"This is it," declared Old King Brady. "I see my blunder now."

"Hist!" whispered Harry. "There's a man on the pier."

So there was, and he was looking over the side, calling down to someone in the water.

The Bradys and Alice, who were still a good distance away, hurried on.

Suddenly the man straightened up and gave a wild start.

They saw him reach to his hip pocket for a revolver.

Before he was able to draw it a shot rang out.

"Heavens! That fellow has picked up one!" Harry cried.

The man flung up his hands, staggered back and fell upon the pier.

"Just in time to be witnesses to a murder!" cried Alice. "Can he be a Chinaman?"

"I couldn't make out," replied Old King Brady. "He must have been shot from a boat, whoever he is."

Their curiosity was now fully aroused, and they lost no time getting on the pier.

No one else seemed to have been attracted by the shot.

In fact, there was only one house to be seen, a small cottage up a lane behind the pier, in the window of which a light burned.

And now the detectives made a discovery which brought them to the conclusion that after all they had made no mistake in starting out to follow up their Chinese clew.

For the man on the pier was a Chinese in American dress.

He was dying when the Bradys came up.

Old King Brady knelt beside him.

"Your name! Who shot you?" he demanded.

The rapidly glazing eyes fixed themselves upon the old detective.

"You—are—Old—King—Brady?" was slowly said.

"Yes, yes! Speak! Are you Pow Chow?"

"Yes. Tell—my—wife."

"It shall be done. Who shot you?"

"Dock Hing—get him."

"If I can."

"Money. I——"

That was all.

Pow Chow breathed his last then.

The Bradys had come up with the crooked mission worker all too late.

Meanwhile Harry and Alice were making discoveries.

On the pier were clothes, evidently belonging to a young man.

When he came to look them over later, Harry recognized the suit which Ed Butler had worn.

But just then their attention was attracted to a stout boat, which was being rapidly pulled out on the Sound.

There were three persons in it, and it could be seen, dark as it was, that one of them wore no clothes.

Harry turned his glass upon the outfit.

It was all he could do, for the boat was already beyond revolver range.

"Chinks," he said. "The naked one is a boy."

"Can it be your Ed?" demanded Alice.

"I can't make out. They are pushing him down into the bottom of the boat. I think they mean to throw him overboard."

"If we had only turned up a few minutes sooner!"

"Yes; it is to be regretted that we didn't.... We can't do a thing as it is."

But the boy was not thrown over.

The last they saw of him he was still lying in the bottom of the boat.

Harry wondered if he was dead.

18

Pow Chow was by this time.

Old King Brady called to them and informed them of the fact.

Then the identifying of Ed's clothes followed.

"We are on deck too late," declared Old King Brady. "If a dying man's word can be believed, those rascals have made off with the money, so, Master Harry, my Chinese clew seems to have amounted to something after all."

They now searched the clothes.

There was nothing in Ed's pockets to identify him, but Harry was certain that these were his clothes.

With Pow Chow it was different.

A memorandum book was discovered in his trousers pocket with his name written on the fly leaf in English.

Better still, twenty-eight hundred dollars in cash turned up.

"Mr. Butler's stolen money, what there is left of it!" Old King Brady exclaimed.

"The wife can't be far away," remarked Alice.

"I judge not from his dying words," replied the old detective. "It is up to us to find her. That must be our job now. It looks as if we were going to be able to close up our case, in part, at least. Let us go on to that lane where we see the light."

## CHAPTER VI.
### ED GETS THE TIN CASE, AND THE CHINKS GET ED.

Did Ed find the crooked pension agent's buried treasure?

That we must now proceed to show.

The Albany boy made a long dive and came up at some distance away from the pier.

Treading water, he peered in beneath it, and seeing no one, swam in closer, for it was very dark.

Pow Chow watched him admiringly.

"See any one under there, Eddie?" he called, assuming that the boy had seen no one or he would have spoken before.

"No, I can't make out that there is any one there," replied Ed, "but I am going to make sure."

"No, no! Don't go in under there. You will play yourself all out. You can see pretty well, can't you?"

Ed got hold of a cross-bar nailed to the piles, and looked long and closely.

His eyes having become accustomed to the gloom, it seemed to him that he could see all there was to be seen.

"No one there," he announced. "I'm going down now, Pow."

"Can you see down there in the dark? You can't. I ought to have thought of that. We can do nothing. I'm a fool."

"I can feel around," replied Ed. "That's all I expected to do. If it is anywhere near the pile I'll find it."

"But you can't stay down long enough."

"Yes, I can."

"How are you going to dive down without coming up on the pier?"

"Great Scott! I know my business. I'm going to swim down."

"Gee, Eddie, you're a wonder!" the Chinaman exclaimed.

Ed leaped up almost clear of the water, he was so nimble, turned a half somersault and made his dive after having located the right pile.

It seemed to Pow Chow as if he was gone an age, and he had almost given the boy up when he at last appeared.

Little did the yellow rascal imagine that he himself would be gone for good before many minutes had passed.

"Well, did you find it?" he cried.

"No," panted Ed. "I worked on the bottom all around the base of the pile, but I couldn't find a thing."

"Too bad! Some one must have got it."

"More than likely after all these years. I'm coming out to get my wind."

There was a standing ladder near by. Ed swam for it and climbed upon the pier, where he sat down on the stringpiece to rest.

"Are you sure you have got the right side of the pier, Pow?" he asked.

"Yes, it is the north side. The paper distinctly says so."

"Well, that was the seventh pile, all right. I can't believe the case is there."

"We ought to try it by daylight," said the Chinaman. "Suppose we ring off and come back in the early morning, Eddie?"

"That's what we shall have to do, I guess. Still, one couldn't see much down there anyhow without a light. That's what we ought to have."

"Are there electric lights made for the use of divers?"

"Sure."

"Well, if we don't succeed I'll buy one, no matter what it costs. I don't propose to give this thing up for two or three days anyhow. But you will try it again, Eddie?" he added persuasively.

"Oh, yes," replied Ed. "I don't mind trying it again, but say, Pow, does the paper tell which end of the pier to count the piles from?"

"Why, no, it don't."

"Which end did you count from?"

"The outside end."

"Suppose I try it at the seventh pile, counting from the inside end?"

"Well, that's an idea. Suppose you do."

Pow Chow now counted the piles from the other end.

No. 7 figured this way came in an entirely different spot.

Rested now, Ed dove again.

At last he came up out of the water, swam to the standing ladder, and holding on, called:

"Well, there is something there!"

"Good! Good!" cried the Chinaman, greatly excited. "Is it a tin case?"

"I think so. It's metal of some kind."

"Why didn't you bring it up?"

"I couldn't unhitch the stone. It is tied fast to a rope."

"You don't say! Eddie, we are going to get it all right."

"It looks so. I'll try it again in a minute. This time I guess I shall be able to unhitch the stone all right."

"Better take down a knife and cut the rope."

"I will if I have to, but it will hamper me. I'd sooner try it the other way first."

Now Ed was not giving out the facts of his discovery straight.

He had not only found one tin case down there, but two.

They were exactly alike, and both had a rope attached to a small ring, the other end being fastened around a stone.

One of these stones the boy had already unhitched.

He knew that he could not successfully handle both cases, although they were by no means bulky.

He did not bring the one he had detached up, because he wanted time to think.

There seemed but one way out of it.

He must abandon his clothes if he wanted to escape from Pow Chow with the money.

Disagreeable as this prospect seemed, Ed determined to risk it and to swim off as soon as he came to the surface.

But a few minutes' reflection changed that.

"I'll come up under the pier and lie low," he said to himself. "He'll think I'm drowned. Mebbe he'll leave my clothes there and I can get them later. If I swim off he'll carry them away sure."

This seemed better than the first plan.

Ed climbed upon the pier for another dive.

Pow Chow questioned him closely.

"We are going to get it, Eddie!" he exclaimed. "We are going to get it, surest thing. If the money is there all right we will all take the first train for San Francisco. Cut out Albany. Your father is half dead, and you don't care for your mother anyway. Come along with us and I'll make a man of you. What do you say?"

"Well, mebbe I will," replied Ed, willing to fool the fellow now that he felt he had got the game in his own hands.

Again he dove.

Descending to the base of the pile, he made his capture.

"Had the money been divided into two parcels?" he asked himself.

He could account for the presence of the two cases in no other way, and yet according to Pow Chow the paper mentioned only one.

Clutching his prize, Ed swam in and rose to the surface under the pier as he had expected.

He looked around for something to hold on to, but it was too dark to see much.

Swimming forward among the piles a few feet, he was suddenly startled by seeing a large boat right ahead of him.

At first he thought he could see a man pull down out of sight into the bottom of the boat.

Treading water and looking again, he could see nobody.

Doubtful what to do, Ed called in a low voice:

"Hello, there! Hello, the boat!"

There was no answer. No one raised up in the boat.

"Strange I didn't see that boat before," muttered Ed. "It must just be tied up under here. There can't be anyone in it or they would have shown themselves by this time. I'll go for it."

He had succeeded in convincing himself that the boat was empty.

Such is the reasoning of a boy; such the chances a boy takes.

For Ed it was a great big miss.

He reached the boat, clutched the gunwale, which was unusually high, and throwing in the case, pulled himself up.

Instantly strong hands clutched him, and he was pulled down on top of two men. Ed was terribly frightened.

So certain was he that he was making no mistake that he had taken almost no precaution towards the last.

The men got him by the throat, punched his head, kicked him and choked him till he was subdued.

Meanwhile Ed made noise enough for Pow Chow to hear.

The Chinaman probably heard something else, too—the boat pulling out from under the pier.

Doubtless that was the time the Bradys saw him bending over the stringpiece.

Ed heard him.

"Eddie! Eddie!" he called. "What's the matter, Eddie? Speak!"

Then a shot rang out.

Ed, who was just picking himself up, saw now that the men were both Chinese.

One worked the oars, the other held a smoking revolver.

They gabbled to each other in Chinese.

Ed was half frightened to death as he got up on the seat.

He could see people running towards the pier, but he could see nothing of Pow Chow.

"They've shot him!" he thought. "Well, I don't care so much, but what will they do with me?"

Just now they were paying little heed to him.

Ed determined to tumble overboard.

But at this he was caught.

21

That was the time the Bradys saw the two Chinamen attack the boy and tumble him into the bottom of the boat.

Ed fought and struggled, but the Chinaman with the revolver pressed the weapon against his naked left breast and gruffly ordered him to keep still unless he wanted to be killed.

Completely cowed now, Ed made no further resistance.

He felt that he had made but a poor exchange.

He wished now that he had played fair with Pow Chow, as well he might.

By this time they were well out on the Sound.

The two Chinks talked incessantly, but of course Ed could make nothing of what they were saying.

In spite of their distance from shore, Ed would have taken to the water but for the revolver which the Chinaman never moved.

At last the other shipped his oars, and producing a rope, proceeded to tie Ed's hands behind him, tumbling the boy about as roughly as if he had been a wooden block.

This done, he picked up the case, and with a small hammer and a little cold chisel proceeded to attack it.

Ed watched him curiously.

At last the lid was pried off and the critical moment came.

As the Chinaman looked into the case he threw it down in disgust.

More hinging and hanging—the same old Chinese gabble so tiresome to a white man's ears.

The other picked up the case and proceeded to examine its contents.

A number of sheets of paper covered with writing came out, and that was all.

Ed did not need to understand Chinese to know how disgusted these two yellow scamps were.

They gabbled on.

One was about to throw the case overboard, but the other prevented him.

This was the man with the revolver—he had put up his weapon now.

"Get up," he said to Ed.

"Can't," was the reply.

The Chinaman soon settled that.

Clutching the naked boy by the hair, he lifted him upon the seat and then thrust the papers upon him.

"What dlese?" he demanded.

"I can't see to read," growled Ed.

The Chinaman settled that, too.

Producing an electric flash lantern, he turned it on the papers.

Ed now saw that these were pension rolls for the Albany district, dating back ten years.

He was familiar with them, for his father, as we have said, was employed in the pension office and handled just such rolls.

Ed tried to explain, and the Chinaman seemed to understand.

"When you fishee dlis up you see noder box dlown dlere in water?" he demanded.

"No," replied Ed.

"Boy, you tellee big lie. Lookee out! Me shootee you! Me tlow you overboard—see?"

Out came the revolver again.

It looked as if the Chink meant what he said.

We must confess that Ed might have held out a little longer.

He gave right up, however, and admitted that there was another box.

"Me knew it!" cried the Chinaman triumphantly. "Yair, dlat it. Him puttee plaper one box, money in noder box. Yair! Bad job you no blingee two blox up out of water. Yair."

Ed was not so sure.

He felt, however, that by holding out the possibility of recovering the other case he had saved his life.

Perhaps it was so.

The other Chink now picked up his oars and pulled steadily on.

The two talked and talked.

At length he of the revolver turned to Ed again.

"Boy, you bully good swim," he said. "Me see you go down one, two, tlee time. Yair."

"I can swim all right," growled Ed.

"Yair. Dlat so. You swimee for me moller night?"

"I suppose I shall have to if you wish me."

"Yair. Me makee. Pow Chow him dlead. Me good flend you now allee light. You gettee box moller. Me givee you whole lot money—see?"

Ed made no answer, not knowing what to say.

Whether this angered the Chinaman or whether he intended to do it anyway, he suddenly pounced upon Ed and caught him by the throat.

Holding him so with one hand, with the other he produced a little vial, drew the cork with his teeth and forced Ed to swallow a portion of the contents of the bottle.

Probably it was knockout drops.

At all events, in a few minutes Ed keeled over and knew no more.

## CHAPTER VII.
### THE FATE OF AN INFORMER.

And after all these efforts the Bradys seemed to have accomplished nothing more than to find themselves with a dead Chinaman on their hands, besides the recovery of the cash.

"What are we to do?" demanded Harry when at last they had finished their examination and talk.

"I suppose we may as well go for the girl," said Old King Brady. "That's our job, I believe."

"And to recover the money and the papers."

"The money we have already got; the papers, I think, will come; perhaps they may prove useless now. The boy has evidently been diving for the treasure. Very likely he has recovered it. Hard to say."

"And this dead Chink?"

"All we can do is to report his presence here to the police, but I shall not be in a hurry. I don't propose to let this lump of dead flesh interfere with the progress of our case."

Thus saying, Old King Brady started up the pier.

He was disgusted to think that he had been just too late.

Still it was something to have recovered the money.

As for Ed, the old detective was not so anxious now.

It looked to him somewhat as if the boy might have gone in with Pow Chow on the deal.

Still he was determined to find Ed, for he felt sure that he had been carried off by the two Chinamen against his will.

They all advanced to the cottage now.

The house was dark save for a light in the kitchen window burning behind a drawn shade.

Old King Brady rapped smartly on the door.

There was a stir inside immediately.

Ethel had been told by her husband how to say in Chinese, "Is that you, Pow?" and the answer was to be in Chinese before she opened the door.

She said it.

Alice caught on to the situation.

"Yes, it is Pow," she answered, imitating a man's voice, which she is perfectly able to do.

Ethel was fooled and she opened the door.

Evidently she had received a description of the old detective, for she drew back, breathing his name.

Then she tried to shut the door, but Harry prevented that with his foot.

"Hold on, Mrs. Pow Wow! We have something to tell you, ma'am!" Old King Brady exclaimed.

"My name is not Pow Wow! It is Pow Chow, and it is as good as any other name!" flashed Ethel. "You go on about your business, you horrid old man. I just won't go back to Albany! I'll marry as many Chinamen as I choose."

"You better not marry more than one at a time unless you want to get arrested for bigamy," replied the old detective dryly as he pushed his way inside.

Ethel ordered them back and began to scream.

"Wait!" said Old King Brady. "You want to stop that noise. We aren't going to murder you. What's more, you have something real to cry for if you really love that Chinese husband of yours."

Evidently she did.

Ethel went into wild hysterics when Old King Brady broke the news to her.

It was easy to see that her grief was real even if afterward it should not prove to have been so very deep.

It took time to quiet her down and get her to the talking point.

At first Ethel refused to talk.

"Look here," said Old King Brady, "it's one of two things. Either we turn you over to your mother, who is in town, or we turn you over to the police. It is up to you."

This settled it.

"I'll talk if I can see my husband—if I know that he is really dead," Ethel then said.

But she talked before that, told all she knew, and gave up the papers.

The briefest kind of an examination was all that was needed to confirm the Bradys' Chinese clew.

Old Fen Wix had told the truth.

Ethel also told about the two Chinamen whom she had seen lurking outside the cottage.

The case seemed plain.

Ed had got the tin case, presumably containing the defaulting pension agent's treasure, and these two Chinks had got Ed.

"This throws our case back into Chinatown," observed Old King Brady. "But we must clean up here first."

They took Mrs. Pow to the pier.

Here there was another scene.

She wanted the Bradys to carry the remains to the cottage.

Old King Brady made her understand that this was impossible until the coroner had viewed them.

They went to the nearest station then and put it up to a police sergeant, explaining nothing further than that a dead Chinaman had been found on the pier; that they had seen two other Chinamen pulling away in a boat, and that Mrs. Pow had identified the dead man.

Then for lack of a better plan the Bradys took Mrs. Pow to their own home, where Alice remained with her until morning, when her mother was telegraphed to come and get her.

Harry and Alice remained behind to wait for the woman, while Old King Brady went to the office.

He was glad he did so, for upon arriving who should he find waiting for him but Mr. Clemmens, the New York Secret Service Commissioner.

"Look here, Brady, you are working up a case for an employee in the Albany pension office, are you not?" Mr. Clemmens asked.

"I am," was the reply.

"A man named Butler?"

"Yes."

"He died last night."

"Indeed?"

"Yes."

"Of what?"

"He has been an invalid for a long time, it seems; heart trouble. When the doctors told him he couldn't live, he sent for the Secret Service Commissioner at Albany and told him a weird story about finding hidden papers relating to the Bradford defalcation in the Albany pension office ten years ago. Said that he meant to give up the money if he succeeded in getting it, but this is doubtful they think up there. At all events, he gave the whole thing away when he found he was dying."

"Did he then!" cried Old King Brady. "Did he say anything about his wife?"

"Yes, that she had run away from him and was after the treasure on her own account. His stepdaughter ran away with a Chinaman and stole the papers."

"That's my case all right," said Old King Brady. "We may as well compare notes."

They did so and the result was some excitement on Mr. Clemmens' part.

He had not altogether believed the story, it seemed.

He immediately called up the Secret Service Bureau at Washington and made a full report of the matter.

They had already heard of it from Albany it appeared.

The result was Old King Brady received orders to go ahead and wind up the case as speedily as possible.

The old detective now did some talking on his own account, wanting to know what he should do with Mrs. Butler and Ethel.

His advice was asked, and it was to drop them as he could not see that it would pay to do otherwise, and this he was told to do.

Thus it became a necessity to finish up the case.

Mr. Clemmens left, and shortly afterward Harry and Alice came in.

Mrs. Butler had called, it appeared.

There had been a pretty hot scene between the pair, after which they went away together.

"Let them bury their dead and go about their business," said Old King Brady. "Meanwhile we will go after the boy and the cash."

"If the boy still lives," observed Harry.

"Even so," was the reply; "the chances are those Chinks knocked him over the head and threw him into the Sound. I am free to confess that I have very little hope of finding him alive."

And such was the latest turn in this singular case.

The question now was what should be the first move.

"What we want is another Chinese clew," said Old King Brady. "You two look up Fen Wix and see what he can do to help us out. You may promise him an extra hundred if necessary. I shall be busy with other matters this morning. I'll look in at the room at three o'clock precisely."

They left.

At three o'clock, when Old King Brady turned up at the room, he found Alice there alone looking very grave.

"Well, what's the matter now?" he demanded.

"I am sorry to tell you that the Chinamen have got Harry," was the reply.

"Got him!"

"Yes."

"How?"

"We went to that address Fen Wix gave and found another old Chink there. He said that Fen Wix had gone to Newark and wouldn't be back till two o'clock."

"And you went again to fall into trouble?"

"That's it."

"Same old Chinatown. How in the world did it happen?"

"Why, when we got there——"

"Where is there, Alice?"

"On Mott street."

"I had forgotten. Well?"

"We knocked several times. Receiving no answer, Harry tried the door and found it unfastened. To our surprise the room had been entirely cleaned out between our visits. There wasn't a stick of furniture in the place."

"Fen Wix must have got himself into trouble through his informing."

"It looks so. Of course, Harry began rubbering around."

"And you, too?"

"Naturally. While we were at it I heard a knock on the door. I had made up half Chinese, as I was before, and thinking that my services as an interpreter would be required, I went to the door. No one was outside. I stepped along the hall and looked over the banisters, but could not see any one."

"And when you went back into the room Harry had vanished, I suppose?"

"You anticipate the ending of my story, Mr. Brady; that was precisely it."

"Same old Chinatown," repeated Old King Brady. "If I had my way I should never touch another case down here. But let us go around there, Alice, and see what we can find. Not that I hope to make much out of it, but something has to be done."

Alice was greatly disturbed and not a little chagrined.

The fact is Harry is her devoted lover, and some day they expect to be married.

More than that, she knows the danger of Chinatown only too well.

The house was one of the old tenements on Mott street which had been provided with extensions and raised up several stories.

The rooms were numbered, and the number of the room given by old Fen Wix was on the third floor.

The door proved to be still unfastened as Alice had left it, and with Old King Brady she entered the vacant room.

Here there was considerable rubbish strewn about, which bore evidence of the hasty move.

"And now for the secret panel," said Old King Brady. "It does beat the cars how the Chinks make those things. Probably there is an entrance here into the secret dens of Pell street."

The search began.

The work was such as Old King Brady is most expert at, and it was not long before he had unearthed a secret panel, but it certainly did not look as if it could be the right one.

For it opened upon what seemed to be just a dumbwaiter shaft.

A rope running over a pulley hung down into it; there was no ladder or stairs.

Old King Brady pulled on the rope.

"There seems to be nothing attached to this," he declared.

And so it proved.

When he got the end of the rope up he found that it had been severed with a sharp knife, and the cut looked to be quite fresh.

"Another Chinese mystery," observed Alice.

"No mystery about this business," was the reply. "Our coming has been anticipated, that's all. This means has been taken to head us off. It is plain enough."

"Perhaps there is another panel, Mr. Brady."

"It would be no surprise to me if we found a dozen of them, but, incidentally, Alice, I have been rather stupid."

"How do you mean?"

"Why, this rope works two ways, and I have only pulled one way. Now I propose to proceed to pull the other. Ha! the rope is weighted at the other end!"

Not only that, but the weight was good and heavy.

It was more than Old King Brady wanted to do to pull it up alone.

Alice took hold to help.

Whatever the weight was they could hear it striking the sides of the narrow shaft with a peculiar dull thud.

It both felt and sounded like a human body, and it made Alice fairly sick, for, of course, she could not help thinking of Harry.

"Here! You let go! You'll faint next," muttered Old King Brady.

26

He was able to read her thoughts.

Indeed, Alice was as white as a sheet.

"Oh, Mr. Brady, do you think it can be poor Harry?" she gasped, continuing to pull.

"Nonsense! Nonsense!" retorted the old detective.

But although he would not admit it, he did think it was Harry just the same.

They kept on pulling, and in a moment the strain was over.

The thing which came up at the end of the rope was, indeed, a human body.

But it was not Young King Brady.

The old detective and Alice found themselves gazing upon the ugly face of Fen Wix.

The rope was tight around his neck—the old man was dead.

"Thank heaven! Not Harry!" gasped Alice.

"I told you so," replied Old King Brady. "Well, well! These Chinese make quick work. And such is the fate of our informer!"

## CHAPTER VIII.
### A PRISONER IN THE SECRET DENS OF PELL STREET.

If Harry was not hung there in that shaft, where then was he?

This must now be explained.

There were two secret panels in that room, as Alice had suggested.

Harry got into the other one.

They caught him suddenly from behind.

The Chinamen, we mean.

He did not see them; he did not hear them. The first he knew a hand was clapped over his mouth and some fearful thing clutched his throat.

It was nothing less than a big pair of nippers which seemed to have been constructed for that very purpose, so well did they suit it.

Harry thought he was a goner.

He could not cry out at first on account of the hand.

The next instant the nippers had him—he could not even turn.

He was dragged backward and knew that he was going through a secret panel near the chimney breast.

Two Chinamen had him captured.

Behind the panel was a shallow space, but it was wide enough for them to stand three abreast.

This trap had been most cleverly constructed.

One of the Chinks pulled a handle and the floor began to descend.

Half strangled, Harry almost lost consciousness, and his head fell forward.

Evidently his tormentors did not intend to go but just so far for immediately the pressure was relaxed.

For a moment things seemed dim and misty.

When Young King Brady recovered himself he was standing in an underground passage leaning against the wall.

Three Chinamen were with him now.

In the third, who held a revolver, Harry recognized a man whom he knew.

It was one Joe Ding, a notorious highbinder.

Only a few months before the Bradys had captured him in connection with a tong shooting affray.

As there did not seem to be much evidence to connect the man with the affair, he had been set free, and that at Harry's suggestion.

Joe Ding knew this, and he had expressed the greatest gratitude at the time.

It was something of a relief to recognize him now, nevertheless it is never safe to trust a highbinder, for murder and robbery is their trade.

"So it's you, Brady," said Joe Ding, who, although now in Chinese dress, did not usually appear so, and what is more he spoke as good English as one could wish.

"Joe Ding!" gasped Harry.

"Yes, as you see. What are you doing here?"

"Why do you ask me that question—you who captured me?"

"I didn't capture you, Brady. It was my friends here."

"But why?"

"Oh, they want to ask you a few questions, and as they don't speak English, I must do the asking."

"Hurry up, then. Can't those infernal nippers be taken off my neck?"

Joe Ding seemed to think so, for he now removed them.

"You are trying to find money sunk in the sand, you and Old King Brady, aren't you?" he demanded.

"Who told you that?" asked Harry.

"Do you deny it?"

"I have said what I have to say."

"You answer my question by asking another. It won't help you any, Brady. Believe me, you better do what I tell you if you expect to get out of this scrap alive."

"Would you kill me after what I have done for you, Joe Ding?"

"I might; it is hard to say," replied the Chinaman with a grin. "However, if it is going to help matters along, I'll answer your question. Follow me."

He clutched Harry's arm and led him forward a few feet.

They had now come underneath an open shaft.

Here there was a rope attached to a ring.

Joe Ding tried to untie it, but did not seem to succeed.

Losing his patience, he pulled out his knife and cut the rope in spite of the protest of one of the other Chinks.

Immediately the rope ran up over a pulley above, apparently, and that with great rapidity.

Evidently something heavy was attached to the other end.

Needless to say it was the corpse of Fen Wix, the informer.

It came down into a sort of niche and stood there leaning against the wall.

Harry shuddered as he looked at it.

"So you have hung the old man?" he gasped.

"As you see," replied Joe Ding. "Is he the man who blabbed to Old King Brady about Pow Chow and this treasure business?"

"Now that he is dead I suppose I may as well admit it. Yes, he is the man."

"I thought so! Then we have made no mistake. Hold on a minute, Brady, till I tell my brothers here."

It looked to Harry as if he should probably have to hold on a good many minutes before he got clear of this outfit if he ever did.

He shuddered as he stood there listening to the gabble of the Chinamen, and wondering what his own fate might be.

"I don't know that I have any further questions to ask you now, Brady," said the Chinaman at length. "You may have a few to ask on your own account, however. If so, now is your chance, for I am in the mood to answer any reasonable question as it happens."

"Why have you captured me?" demanded Harry. "That is the main question."

"And it shall be answered. I have captured you on general principles. I know what you Bradys are. Once you put your hand to a case you never let up. I want to give Old King Brady something else to think of, so as to turn his attention away from this treasure business. Naturally he will now turn his attention to finding you, but take my word for it he won't succeed."

"Joe," said Harry, "you take my word for it, you will do well to let me go."

"Wait, Brady, I'll tell you something you don't know by and by," whispered the Chinaman. "I'm doing you a big favor if you only knew it."

He winked and looked wise.

Harry stopped talking then.

He came to the conclusion that one at least of the other Chinks understood English.

It seemed best to fall in with the situation for the present at least.

The usual programme in such cases was now carried out.

Young King Brady was blindfolded and led through passages, up steps and down, in and out until he finally landed in an underground room decently furnished in Chinese style.

There was nothing notable about the room except a handsome gilt scroll hanging against the wall which represented the Chinese dragon. It was really a handsome piece of work.

Here the eye bandage was removed and Harry was left to his own reflections.

They were anything but pleasant, for once again he found himself a prisoner in the secret dens of Pell street.

"But why didn't they take Alice?" he asked himself. "Why was it only me?"

He was soon to learn, if Joe Ding was to be believed, for within an hour the Chinaman came to him alone, unlocking the heavy door behind a pair of portieres which had resisted all Harry's efforts.

He might, indeed, have managed to open it if he had been left his skeleton keys.

But as we should have mentioned, he was searched at the start, and these with his revolver, watch and what money he had about him, were taken away.

The Chinaman locked the door behind him and came forward with a look of mystery on his face.

"I suppose you are feeling very sore toward me, Brady," he said.

"Well, I must admit, Joe, that I am not especially happy," replied Harry. "But what is it you have to say? Let's have it, quick!"

"It's just this," replied the Chinaman, "I've saved your life."

"How do you figure that out?"

"Easy. You have bunked up against one of the most dangerous tongs in Chinatown, and all the more dangerous on account of its being so little known. I refer to the Brotherhood of the Red Door."

"I have known this long time that such a society existed in San Francisco, but I didn't know they had a lodge here in New York."

"Well, they have."

"Are you a member?"

"Now don't go to asking questions. It is enough for you to know that your death has been decreed by this tong. It is the same with Old King Brady. You want to tell him that."

"How can I tell him when I am a prisoner here in this secret den?"

"Wait! You may get out of this. Now let me tell you that I helped capture you for a purpose. I haven't forgotten what you did for me. I persuaded them to lock you up in this room till night. Then they mean to kill you, run your corpse out in a wagon, and dump it into the river, but I am here now to set you free."

Joe Ding seemed sincere.

Harry responded heartily.

Thanking the Chinaman, he promised that he should be well paid if he carried out his plan.

"I hope you will let up on that money business," Joe said. "I warn you, it is at the risk of your lives if you follow it up."

"Look here, Joe," replied Harry, "that's all right. I can only promise to tell Old King Brady what you say. He will do as he pleases, but there was a boy mixed up in that business. What about him? Is he alive or dead?"

"Ask me nothing," replied Joe Ding. "I can tell nothing, nor will I. I am here to help you, and that is just as far as I'm going—see?"

Harry gave up then, as there seemed to be no other way.

Joe Ding now unlocked the door, and telling Harry to wait, went out through the passage and was gone for some moments.

At last he returned and announced that the coast was clear.

"Come along," he added. "If I can only get you safe out on Pell street it is all I ask, but understand one thing, if we are spotted, I beat it. You will have to look out for yourself in that case. I have my own life to save."

"All right," said Harry. "Lead on."

They hurried along the passage and came to a flight of rickety wooden steps.

Joe Ding stopped to listen.

"It is all right," he said. "You don't hear anything, do you?"

"Not a sound."

"Good! Come!"

They started up the steps then.

Joe Ding, we should have mentioned, carried an ordinary lantern.

The Chinaman was ahead, and no sooner had he reached the top of the steps than he ran against trouble.

Instantly three Chinamen rose up from the floor and flung themselves upon him.

Such another snarling scrap for a moment there never was. It was like a cat fight.

Harry jumped in to help.

There was no chance.

The lantern went down and was extinguished.

At the same instant someone came tumbling down the steps.

Whoever it was bowled Harry off his feet and he went down, too.

The man sprang up and chased off along the passage, but poor Harry hit his head as he fell, and half stunned, was slow to rise.

Before he could get on his feet the enemy was upon him.

A flashlight was displayed.

Harry was seized and thrown down again.

There were five Chinks in it now.

Joe Ding was not among them.

Two bent over Young King Brady, one choking him until he was helpless.

Another producing a bottle, forced him to swallow some vile tasting stuff.

This settled it.

Young King Brady's brain quickly began to whirl.

In a very few moments he was unconscious.

Joe Ding's plan had failed.

True to his threat, he promptly "beat it" when trouble came, leaving poor Harry still in the power of the Chinese of the secret dens of Pell street.

## CHAPTER IX.
### ED FALLS INTO NEW HANDS.

It would seem as if the brothers of the Red Door tong were especially addicted to drugging.

Ed got his dose in the boat, as has been told.

When the boy awoke it was not to full consciousness. He felt like one in a dream.

He was lying in the bottom of a boat naked.

An old tarpaulin had been thrown over him, but just then Ed did not realize what it was.

He could feel the motion of the boat as it bobbed about. He could hear the lapping of the waves, but there were no other sounds until at last a steamboat whistle gave a dismal croak.

But each moment served to brighten the boy's brain, until at last he threw off the tarpaulin and sat up.

At first he fancied that he was still in the boat under that pier up in the Bronx.

Dim and misty were his recollections.

It seemed to Ed that the attack by the Chinamen, the shooting of Pow Chow, and all that followed, must have been a dream.

It was certainly the same boat, and there was nobody in it but himself.

A rope made it fast to a pile, it was floating about under the pier.

"I must have hit my head in some way," reasoned Ed. "That's what's the matter. Bless me, don't I feel queer! What strange dreams I have had! I suppose Pow Chow thinks I have been drowned."

He felt now that it was time to act, and he tried to stand up in the boat.

Very quickly Ed found that this would not work.

He was glad to sit down on the seat. If he had not done so he surely would have fallen.

Just then the boat began to move rapidly forward.

Looking, Ed saw that a hand was clutching the rope.

The boat was pulled out from under the pier and Ed saw a tough looking young man clinging to a standing ladder.

"Aw, say," he cried, "youse is come back to business, has you? Come up out of dat now. You must climb de ladder. De Chinks are waitin' for yer—see?"

"I—I can't!" gasped Ed. "I'm too dizzy."

"Yer must!" was the reply.

"But I shall fall into the water."

"No yer won't, and if yer do I'll be behind to ketch yer. Can't stop here without any clothes on—see?"

He jumped into the boat, continuing to urge Ed to make the move, which he presently did.

The man kept close behind him, and it was well that he did, for twice Ed lost his hold.

The fellow supported him, however, and he finally got upon the pier, where he sank down at the feet of two Chinamen.

"I guess youse has doped him half to de't, dat's what's de matter," said the man.

"He comee alle light. He comee lound allee light," chattered one of the Chinamen.

And sure enough, in a few minutes Ed found himself much better.

The other Chink had a suit of Chinese clothes, and he now ordered Ed to dress himself in them, which he was able to do with some help.

By this time the illusion had been dispelled.

Not only were these the same Chinamen, but Ed could see by the lights of the bridges that they were now away downtown, for he had studied the map of New York and he knew about where the bridges were located.

The two Chinamen now led him down the uncovered pier to South street, where an old ramshackle hack was waiting.

Ed got in unresistingly. He was too weak to help himself.

The tough proved to be the driver.

He got on the box, started up his horses and rounded them up in Chinatown.

During the ride Ed dropped off asleep and had to be aroused.

He was so weak and heavy that they had to almost carry him.

They passed through a narrow hallway and went down into a cellar.

Here a trap door was raised and they went still further down.

They were, in fact, descending into the secret dens of Pell street.

Ed was rounded up in a little room where there were several Chinese sleeping on mattresses which had been thrown on the floor.

All were boys. The place was abominably hot and smelled horribly.

There was no mattress for Ed.

He was told to lie down beside a boy who did not even arouse as he dropped upon it.

A moment later Ed was sound asleep.

And he must have slept very soundly—perhaps he was drugged again—for when he awoke he was in a smaller room, lying alone upon a cot-bed.

The room was dimly lighted by a lantern.

Ed found that he had been undressed also. He had nothing on but an old undershirt now.

After lying awake a long time he got up to see how he could stand it on his feet.

He found he was all right; a little shaky, perhaps, but so much better than he had been the night before that he felt that the effects of the drug had practically passed.

He tried the door and found it locked.

Window there was none. Escape thus seemed impossible, but the enterprising Ed did not give up.

He was resolved to know all about his prison before he did that.

In course of his search he took in the ceiling, and there he beheld a trap door.

It fascinated the boy, for it seemed to offer an avenue of escape.

No one coming, Ed resolved to make the attempt to reach it.

He looked around for clothes first, but there were none to be found.

Stripping the cot, he leaned it up against the wall under the trap door and climbed upon it.

He could now reach the trap and had some room to spare. Pushing on it, the door arose and fell back with noise enough to startle any one within hearing.

But evidently there was no one, for nothing happened.

Ed waited several minutes, and at last feeling himself safe, he caught hold and pulled himself up through the opening.

He found himself now in a dark narrow passage so low that he could not stand upright.

The lantern was needed. Why had he forgotten that?

It was necessary to get down on top of the cot again.

Ed made the descent, reached for the lantern, got it and returned.

"I suppose if I do succeed in reaching the street I shall be arrested," he said to himself, "but I don't care. Anything is better than being held a prisoner by these horrible Chinese."

He crept along the passage, which appeared to be of considerable length, at last coming upon three steps leading down to a door.

And now the boy caught the sound of strange music.

Some one was strumming on a banjo.

The tune was most monotonous, just the same thing over and over again.

"Chinese music," thought Ed. "That's one of their big moon banjos. I suppose I may as well go back. I'll only get myself into trouble if I try to butt in here."

But the music seemed to fascinate him, and he found it hard to pull away.

Creeping down the steps, he stood for some moments listening at the keyhole.

Feeling at last as if it really would be better for him to go, he was just about to pull away when, as he turned, the lantern hit hard against the door.

Instantly the music ceased.

Scared, Ed bounded up the steps and retreated along the passage.

But it was no use.

The door flew open and he could hear somebody coming after him.

Feeling that he might as well be caught in the passage as in the act of getting down through the trap door, Ed turned to face his pursuer.

He was a young Chinaman, very much Americanized in appearance.

He, like Ed, was forced to crouch low, and he looked very fierce as he thrust his ugly face forward close under Ed's nose.

"Who are you?" he demanded. "Say, who are you?"

"Don't kill me!" gasped Ed, feeling rather foolish when he had said it.

"Kill you nothing! Why should I kill you? Say, are you Dock Hing's prisoner?"

"I am a prisoner all right. I don't know Dock Hing."

"Listen! Are you the boy what did the diving?"

"Yes."

"Gee! Say, dis is great."

This Chink spoke English with a Bowery accent.

He seemed to be perfectly enraptured to have discovered Ed.

"Who's down dere?" he demanded, pushing past and peering down through the open trap.

"Nobody."

"You sure?"

"Yes."

32

"You were trying to escape."

"I had to do the best I could for myself."

"You come with me, boy. What's your name?"

"Ed Butler."

"Oh, yair! I know! Go ahead dere now. Go now. I'll give you a kick—see?"

Ed traveled on down the steps and through the door.

The Chinaman following shot a bolt and turned to face the boy.

It was just a dingy little bedroom without a window and lighted by an ordinary lamp.

"Sit down," ordered the Chinaman, pointing to a chair.

He picked up a moon banjo out of another, and putting it on the floor sat down himself.

Then a fire of questions was thrown at Ed.

Nobody can ask questions like a Chinaman once he goes at it.

"You dived for that money?" was the first.

"Yes," replied Ed.

"You didn't get it?"

"I got a tin box. There was no money in it—only papers."

"What did they do to you?"

"They drugged me."

"Say, you are lucky to be alive. Dock Hing is a bad one. It's lucky for you that you met me. Say, I'll help you out of dis providin' you tell me de trute, dat is."

"What do you mean?"

"Dock Hing tinks you must have found two tin boxes down dere. Did yer?"

"What if I did?"

"Tell me de trute. We'll go for dat other box and divide. What do yer say?"

"Well, then, if you will have it, Dock Hing is right," Ed said. "I did see another box down there."

"I knowed it!" cried the fellow. "Gee! dis is great. Will you stand in wit me den and get dat box?"

"Yes, I will providing you will get me some clothes and help me to get out of this dreadful place," declared Ed.

"It's a bargain. Now where's de place?"

"That's the trouble," sighed Ed. "I was drugged when they took me there and I was drugged when they brought me away."

"Go ahead and tell me all you know. Mebbe I can dope it out."

Ed went over the few details he possessed.

The Chinaman continued to question him closely.

At last he declared that he felt pretty sure he could find the place.

"We can make a stab at it anyway," he said. "I'm wise. It's in the Bronx above Morris' Docks. We'll get up there to-night."

"And now that we are partners, what's your name?" Ed asked.

"You can call me Tom Quee," replied the Chinaman. "That's what I'm generally called."

It was no encouragement on top of this statement that at the same instant there came a loud knocking at the door.

## CHAPTER X.
### YOUNG KING BRADY IN A BAD WAY.

Old King Brady concluded that the best disposition he could make of what remained of Fen Wix, the informer, was to lower the corpse down again, and this he proceeded to do.

He and Alice then put in a good half hour searching for another secret panel.

They failed to find it.

This left the old detective in no pleasant frame of mind.

"I suppose we have got to get the police, make a raid on this lane and overhaul everything," he declared.

"What about Pell street?" asked Alice. "There are those abandoned secret rooms you were in yesterday. They lie nearly in the rear of this house. There might something come of it if we tried our luck there again."

"I am afraid not, Alice. Harry and I went over that ground pretty thoroughly, still we can try."

"Is it so that I can go in there?"

"I don't know why not. We will get back to the room. You can change to your ordinary dress. Then we will look up the wardman."

"You don't intend to try it alone then?"

"No, I think it will be best for us to have help. No use in mincing matters in this case. There is no telling what we may run up against."

To secure the wardman it was necessary to go, to the Elizabeth street station, something Old King Brady greatly disliked to do, for he hates to have to apply to the police in connection with his own affairs.

He got the help readily enough, however.

With the wardman they went to Pell street and did up such secret dens as they knew about thoroughly.

Nothing came of it.

The rooms were all deserted as the Bradys had found them the previous day.

It was after five o'clock before they finished up their work.

Alice was in despair for it was a very serious case and she could see that the old detective was quite as much concerned as herself.

"What can we do?" she asked.

"Our best plan is to ring off for a few hours," replied Old King Brady.

"But poor Harry?"

"Listen, Alice, if the Chinese meant to kill Harry I need not tell you that by this time they have probably carried their intention into effect. It will do no harm to delay a little. Every move we have made has doubtless been watched and reported to those rascals. Mr. Connors, don't you think I am right?"

"Sure," replied the wardman. "Best thing you can do. You want to report that dead Chink, around on Mott street pretty quick, though."

Old King Brady had told the wardman about Fen Wix's fate, although he said nothing about it at the station.

"Just what I don't want to do," he replied. "Hear my theory. Right away after dark the Chinks will probably make some move in connection with that matter, if they haven't done it already. Opening off that room is a smaller one in which we can hide. If you can stick with us I propose that at about eight o'clock we all get on the job there and see if we can't catch some Chink who will serve us to get the secret of that other panel, which I am satisfied exists."

"Well, that's so. It might work out to the good," replied the wardman. "Anyhow it seems to be our only chance."

"It does, and we will try it," replied the old detective. "And now let us pull out."

Old King Brady and Alice went to the office thinking it barely possible that Harry might have escaped and gone there.

Failing here they went home to supper and at eight o'clock turned up at the Pell street room again.

There was nothing to be found here either, so they waited until Wardman Connors came and then went around on Mott street.

The wardman stepped in first.

It had been arranged that if he found anyone in the room he should come back and inform them; otherwise he was to wait there till they came up.

Giving the man ten minutes, Old King Brady and Alice went up stairs.

Mr. Connors heard them coming and opened the door for them.

"No one here?" questioned Old King Brady.

"No one."

"Is the corpse still fastened to the rope?"

"Sure thing. I didn't attempt to pull it up.'"

It was getting dark.

Old King Brady and the wardman pulled on the rope and brought up old Fen Wix again.

The body was again lowered and Old King Brady and Alice, along with the wardman, took up their stations in the smaller room.

A tedious wait followed, but along towards nine o'clock the patience of the detectives was rewarded by hearing someone enter the other room.

They had left the door slightly ajar and Old King Brady peered through the opening.

A Chinaman in native dress stood there in the dark.

Old King Brady drew his revolver ready for business.

He was not called upon to act, however.

The man went to the other side of the chimney, which Old King Brady had examined with the greatest care.

For a moment he stood there and then he vanished.

Unfortunately as he vanished the old detective could not see just what the fellow did.

"Hush!" breathed Alice as he was about to step out into the other room. "Someone else coming, I think."

But it proved to be only some person passing the door on their way to the floor above.

They went outside after the alarm had passed and again Old King Brady examined that particular piece of wall.

And this time he found it.

The arrangement was very peculiar, but Old King Brady mastered the mystery and the opening stood revealed.

Behind the panel there was a very narrow flight of stairs leading down.

Old King Brady immediately started to descend, flashing his light ahead of him.

They followed him down into the place to which Harry had been taken.

There in the niche stood the corpse of the informer, silent and quiet.

Following the passage for a short distance they came upon two inner doors, both set at an angle.

"Which den do you propose to tackle first?" questioned Connors.

"To the right is always my rule, unless I have reason to change it," replied the old detective.

"To the right it is then," said the wardman.

He tried the door, to find it locked.

So was the door on the left.

Old King Brady got his skeleton keys into business and succeeded in opening the right-hand door.

The usual secret passage, Chinese style, lay behind.

Listening and hearing no sound they cautiously advanced.

The passage was not only narrow but it wound around.

At last they saw a light ahead.

"Coming to something at last," whispered Old King Brady.

They stole on, coming up with the light.

A heavy dear stood open. Behind it were portieres of red cloth, partly drawn. The light came streaming in between these curtains and they could hear voices talking in Chinese inside.

"What are they saying?" Old King Brady breathed in Alice's ear.

"They think someone is dead," whispered Alice. "That is as near as I can make it out."

"Stand ready for business, Connors," said the old detective. "Now for our look."

Old King Brady and Alice, pushing in between the curtains, saw enough.

Harry had got himself into a bad fix.

There he lay on the floor with three Chinamen bending over him.

One held a box, another a long glass vial.

What were they about?

35

Old King Brady did not stop even to try to learn.

Calling to Connors he dashed into the room.

Alice and the wardman equally with himself had their revolvers ready.

Then it was a case of three against three.

Taken entirely by surprise, the Chinks surrendered almost without an attempt at resistance.

The detectives had come prepared with four pairs of handcuffs.

Thus the prisoners were easily secured.

"The man who raises his voice dies," cried Old King Brady. "Mind what I tell you now! I suppose you all understand English, but in case you don't here is one who will tell you in your own language what I have said."

Alice repeated his command in Chinese.

There was no talk made.

Old King Brady then bent over Harry and proceeded to examine into his condition.

It was evident that the young detective had been deeply drugged.

Personally Old King Brady was inclined to consider the case a very serious one, but he restrained himself and kept cool.

"Question them, Alice," he ordered.

Alice obeyed and there was considerable talk.

"Is it opium?" asked the old detective.

"This man says not."

"I wouldn't risk it, Mr. Brady. Better take him to the hospital," said the wardman.

"I think so too," replied the old detective. "You and Alice get the prisoners out, Connors. Telephone for an ambulance. I'll remain on guard here."

It seemed a big risk but there was no other way and this was done.

But in about five minutes a policeman whom they met on Mott street joined Old King Brady.

His presence was hardly needed, however, for no one came.

Alice was back soon after reporting that the three prisoners had been rounded up at the Elizabeth street station and the call for the ambulance given.

## CHAPTER XI.
### ED STILL ON THE JOB.

Tom Quee seemed as much concerned over the sudden knocking on the door as Ed was himself.

"Who can it be?" he breathed.

As Ed did not know he suggested that it might be a good scheme to answer the knock and find out.

"I shall have to do it," whispered Tom Quee as the knocking continued, "but first to get you out of sight. It won't do to have you seen."

Tom Quee opened the door of a closet and pushed Ed inside.

"Don't make a sound if you value your life," he whispered as he closed the door upon him.

An unpleasant half hour followed.

Two Chinamen came into the room.

Tom Quee seemed to have his hands full with them, whatever it was they wanted.

They gabbled away in Chinese until Ed was sick of listening to them.

Then they seemed to fade away.

He ventured to open the door slightly and peer through the crack.

The room was vacant; the door leading into the secret passage was open; evidently the Chinamen had gone that way.

Ed slipped out and tried the other door, seized with some wild idea of making his escape.

There was nothing doing, however, for the door was securely locked and the key gone.

Glad to get back to his closet, Ed waited there.

At last all three Chinamen returned and Tom Quee let the intruders out, calling Ed when they had gone.

"It's all right now," he said. "You can come out. They were looking for you. Your escape has been discovered. They thought you might have come this way, but I fooled 'em. They will trouble us no more. Now is our time to get out of this."

Just who Tom Quee was or how he came to be there in the secret room Ed never learned.

The Chinaman seemed to know the ropes, however.

He provided Ed with clothes and led him through many winding passages, up stairs and down, until at last they came out up in Pell street.

Tom Quee now led the way to the Bowery.

They went up the Bowery, and stopping in at a restaurant the Chinaman put up for a good meal, which Ed was glad enough to get.

As they ate they talked and it was decided to go at once to the Bronx and start their work, which they did.

Ed now resigned himself entirely to the guidance of the Chinaman.

He had little idea where they went. The ride in the subway seemed interminable, and a long ride by trolley car followed.

At last they came to the water front, where there were docks and factories.

It was now night and Ed was almost tired out.

The Chinaman tried to hire a boat but no one he could find would rent him one.

Tom Quee was a persistent fellow, however.

"If we can't hire a boat we must steal one," he said, as they came to a pier. "Let's go down here and see what we can find."

They explored and found that there were three boats fastened to this pier.

Watching his chance Tom Quee slipped down into one of them and Ed followed.

It was now almost nine o'clock in the evening.

The night was singularly hot and oppressive.

The effects of the drug were still on the boy.

He hardly realized it then, but later he understood why he was so indifferent to all that was passing.

When they got out on the water, he grew so sleepy that he could scarcely hold his head up.

"You want to go to sleep," declared the Chinaman. "You can do nothing at all now. Lie down in the bottom of the boat and take a snooze."

Ed was only too glad to obey.

When he awoke it seemed to him as if he must have been sleeping a long time.

The boat was tied up to a pier and Tom Quee had vanished.

Now, if ever, seemed Ed's chance to escape.

Looking around, the place seemed rather familiar, and he soon came to the conclusion that it was the scene of his adventures the night before.

"Where in thunder is the Chinaman?" he asked himself. "What ought I to do?"

His one idea now was to get away and find the detectives if he could.

And yet he could not seem to give up the thought of the pension agent's money either.

Ed sat in the boat hesitating.

He who hesitates is lost, they say.

At all events the boy determined to make another effort to secure the treasure, for he was satisfied that this was, indeed, the same pier.

But what had become of Tom Quee?

That was the question.

It seemed as if he ought to know that first.

Unhitching the boat, Ed pulled to the standing ladder.

Securing the boat here he climbed upon the pier.

The boy, after some further hesitation, descended to the boat again and undressed.

At last having located his seventh pile, Ed took a dive and swam towards it.

Springing up he dove and swam near to the bottom, where he began his search.

It was soon rewarded.

The other box was where he had left it but it had taken longer to locate it than he expected, and it was necessary now to ascend to the surface again.

The boat was where he had left it and Ed swam to it and climbed in.

That he was far from being master of himself even yet was certain.

But he knew enough to stick to his purpose and presently he made another dive and went down again.

And this time he easily secured the other case.

As his head came above the surface of the water Ed saw something which made his heart stand still.

Two Chinamen were peering down over the stringpiece.

They certainly saw him but they instantly pulled back out of sight.

"The same outfit," thought Ed. "They have captured Tom Quee, that's what. Now I am in the soup."

He dropped under the water, thankful that he had not allowed the hand which held the case to come into view.

Swimming under water to the standing ladder he hastily attached the rope, which still remained fastened to the case, to one of the submerged rungs.

Again Ed came to the surface and all breathless from his exertions, climbed into the boat.

And now again the boy ventured to look up, but he could see nothing of the two Chinamen.

"They are on the job all right though," thought Ed, "and they are watching me now. What on earth shall I do?"

It was indeed a problem.

Sitting quiet for a few minutes, Ed began to dress.

He had no sooner got the undershirt on which Tom Quee had provided for him than the two Chinks appeared at the top of the standing ladder.

"Hello, boy!" called one. "You gettee dlat blox?"

It was Dock Hing all right and he held a big revolver in his hand.

Ed was in despair.

"You again!" he gasped.

"Yair! Me comee 'gain," chuckled Dock Hing, and he came down the ladder, his companion holding Ed covered while Hing descended.

The other came down after him.

Ed was a prisoner once more.

"You gettee blox?" demanded Dock Hing.

"Whatever happens, you shan't get it," thought Ed, and so he denied it.

"You lie," said Dock Hing. "You go dlown into water twice. Me see you. Me tlink you gettee blox."

"No!" persisted Ed. "There is no box."

The Chinaman laughed softly.

"Allee light," he said. "Dlen you dlive again and again and again till you gettee blox, see?"

"It's no use," declared Ed. "There is no box, I tell you. I've looked and I can't find it."

They did not mention Tom Quee. They never asked him how he came to be there.

All they seemed interested in was the box. "You dive again," ordered Dock Hing. "Come now, you be good boy and we give you money so we find money in blox, see?"

He ordered Ed to take off his shirt and make another dive.

There was no help for it.

"This time I'll give them the slip," thought Ed, and as he dove he swam away under the pier, coming up on the other side.

But the wily Chinks were too many for the boy.

38

As he rose to the surface a voice called, and looking up he saw Dock Hing grinning down over the stringpiece.

"Go back!" cried the Chinaman. "Go back or me shootee you. Go back, you little flaud."

They were everywhere.

Ed was in despair.

Yielding to the inevitable he turned and swam back under the pier.

## CHAPTER XII.
## CONCLUSION.

Old King Brady thought that Harry was dead.

They carried him out of the secret door only with the greatest difficulty.

The worst was when it came to getting Harry up the narrow stairs, but even this was managed and they landed him in the ambulance at last.

The young doctor in charge lent them little encouragement.

"He is certainly gone, Mr. Brady," he said as he looked Harry over. "I wish I could hold out more hope to you, but I can't."

Alice, who was in the ambulance, suddenly turned to the old detective and said:

"Really, Mr. Brady, it is useless to take Harry to the hospital. If he is not dead now he will die before he gets there. The only possible chance to save him is to get a Chinese doctor."

"Nonsense!" mused the ambulance surgeon. "What do Chinese doctors know? They are the worst kind of quacks."

"Why, no."

"Don't be in such a hurry to pronounce on what you don't understand. Alice, your suggestion is a good one. Doctor, we will take my partner to No. —— Chatham Square."

The place to which Old King Brady prepared to take Harry was Quong Lee's opium joint.

This is located in a basement on Chatham Square.

Quong Lee, who is a man advanced in years, reckons himself a particular friend of the old detective.

Alice went in first and saw Quong Lee, coming out with word that they were to bring Harry right in.

"I am going for the doctor," she said. "He has given me the address."

She hurried away, leaving Old King Brady to assist in carrying Harry down the stone steps.

Quong Lee was on hand at the foot. "Bling him to my loom," he said and he led the way.

And once again poor Harry had to be dragged up a flight of narrow stairs.

When they got him on Quong Lee's bed and loosened up his clothes the old divekeeper made a personal examination.

"What do you think, Quong?" demanded Old King Brady when at last he pulled away.

"Him velly bad," was the reply. "Me muchee flaid, Blady."

"You consider him dead?"

Quong Lee nodded.

It was despairing, but as the old detective had already come to the same conclusion he said nothing and at last the Chinese doctor came.

Instead of being the old man they had expected to see, he was quite a youthful looking proposition.

Moreover, he wore American clothes and spoke perfect English.

His name was High Lung, he informed Old King Brady.

"There's your patient, Doctor," said the old detective. "He has been drugged by some of your people. To me he seems dead. Save him if you can and I'll write you a check for a thousand dollars."

39

High Lung made no answer but proceeded to examine Harry.

He took a long time about it, too. Old King Brady began to think he never would let up.

At last Dr. High Lung pulled away.

"He is not dead," he said, quietly. "I can save him."

"Good!" cried Old King Brady. "Go ahead."

High Lung then ordered Alice from the room and Harry was stripped.

The Chinese doctor's treatment certainly was peculiar at the start.

He climbed in the bed and lay down flat on top of Harry, breathing in his mouth and at the same time kneading his back with his hands.

The ambulance surgeon looked on with no attempt to conceal his disgust.

At last the Chinaman got off the bed and began opening a bag which he had brought along.

"Examine him now, Doctor," he said.

The surgeon did so.

"Upon my word it is a fact that he is breathing," he admitted. "I wouldn't have believed it."

The Chinese doctor then produced just such another box and vial as the old detective had seen the Chinamen handling in the secret den.

Calling for a cup he put into it a portion of a grayish powder out of the box and poured a bright blue liquid upon it out of the vial.

The mixture immediately foamed up.

"Doctor, do you know the drug which has been used on my partner?" asked Old King Brady.

"Perfectly well," replied the doctor.

"Does it act on the heart?" demanded the surgeon.

"Both on the heart and lungs," was the reply, and this was all they could get out of High Lung, who now proceeded to administer the mixture to Harry.

It promptly did its work. Within ten minutes Young King Brady opened his eyes.

"Oh! I have had such queer dreams!" he muttered.

"Dream some more," said High Lung; and taking Old King Brady aside he said:

"They gave him an overdose. He was almost gone. He must not be moved out of here under two days. I shall want to see him twice again."

"The case is yours," said Old King Brady. "I shall stay right here with him."

But he did not.

Harry here spoke again.

"Governor," he said, "you want to get right up to that pier. Never mind me. I dreamed that I saw you there and that you got—you know what. Go now."

And Harry was so earnest about it that Old King Brady went, leaving him in charge of Alice and Quong Lee.

It was well towards midnight before Old King Brady again found himself approaching the old fertilizer factory.

He was not alone.

Feeling that he might need help he confided the details of his case to Wardman Connors and took him along.

"I don't see a soul," remarked Connors as they approached the pier. "I am afraid it is all Harry's imagination."

They started down the pier and had gone but a short distance before they made a discovery.

It was a Chinaman lying gagged and bound upon the pier.

"Why, I know this Chink!" exclaimed Connors. "He is a notorious Pell street highbinder. Name is Tom Quee."

The imprisoned Chinaman was regarding him with a disgusted stare.

They set him free at once and Connors started to question him.

"Know Dock Hing?" said Tom Quee. "Well, he did it. He's hanging around here somewhere in a boat along with another fellow."

40

"Why?" demanded Old King Brady.

"I don't know," retorted Tom Quee. "We had a quarrel—that's all."

They started across the pier thinking that Tom Quee would follow them.

Suddenly they heard the patter of feet and looking back saw the Chinaman on the run.

They went on the stringpiece then, making as little noise as possible.

Looking down they saw a boat at some distance ahead in which sat two Chinamen.

They were looking down into the water.

"Sure enough they are the men now!" muttered Old King Brady. "Connors, these are the ones we want. Upon my soul I believe that boy is diving for them now."

He was right.

At the same moment up came Ed out of the water.

He was empty-handed.

One of the Chinamen seized an oar and would have struck at him but Old King Brady raised a shout.

The Chinamen looking up and seeing the detectives, instantly pulled their boat in under the pier.

"That you, Ed Butler?" cried Old King Brady, hurrying forward. "Oh, Mr. Brady! I'm so thankful you have come!" Ed cried. "I've had such a time of it since I parted with you."

"There go the Chinks!" exclaimed Connors, pointing to the boat which was pulling away from the pier.

"I found two metal cases down there. One last night those Chinamen opened. There was nothing in it but a lot of papers," said Ed.

"And the other?"

"That I got to-night, and oh, Mr. Brady, I have had the time of my life to keep it out of the hands of those Chinamen."

"But where is it now?" demanded the old detective impatiently.

"I tied it to the lowest rung of that ladder under the water," said Ed.

"Go for it!" cried the old detective. "Don't keep us any longer in suspense."

Ed instantly took a header into the water.

Ed's head came popping up in a minute.

He raised a hand out of the water and it held a square tin case, with a rope attached.

"It's the duplicate of the one I fetched up last night," he said. "I don't know what's in it, I'm sure."

"Bring it up here and we'll soon find out," called Old King Brady.

Ed came up with his prize, but it was not so easy settling the all important question after all.

Old King Brady had all kinds of trouble opening the thing, but at last the lid was pried back, and sure enough money was revealed.

It proved to be the Albany pension money and the Government got it.

Old King Brady saw to it that Ed came in for a share of the reward. The boy went back to Albany but his mother and Ethel failed to return. The last Ed heard of them they were in San Francisco, where the misguided girl had married another Chinaman.

Harry was under the weather for a week but he entirely recovered and wants nothing more to do with the secret dens of Pell street.

And thus the case was rushed to a successful finish the night following up the Brady's Chinese Clew.

### THE END.

Read "THE BRADYS IN A FOG; OR, TRACKING A GANG OF FORGERS," which will be the next number (605) of "Secret Service."

SPECIAL NOTICE:—All back numbers of this weekly, except the following, are in print: 1 to 6, 9, 13, 42, 46, 47, 53 to 56, 63, 81. If you cannot obtain the ones you want from any newsdealer send the price in money or postage stamps by mail to FRANK TOUSEY,

Publisher, 24 Union Square, New York City, and you will receive the copies you order by return mail.

SECRET SERVICE

NEW YORK, AUGUST 19, 1910.

TERMS TO SUBSCRIBERS

Single Copies .25 CentsOne Copy Three Months .65 CentsOne Copy Six Months $1.25One Copy One Year $2.50

Postage Free.

HOW TO SEND MONEY—At our risk send P. O. Money Order, Check, or Registered Letter; remittances in any other way are at your risk. We accept Postage Stamps the same as cash. When sending silver wrap the Coin in a separate piece of paper to avoid cutting the envelope. *Write your name and address plainly. Address letters to*

SINCLAIR TOUSEY, President } Frank Tousey, PublisherGEO. G. HASTINGS, Treasurer } 24 Union Sq., New YorkCHAS. E. NELAUREL, Secretary}

## ITEMS WORTH READING.

Mrs. Guy Wood went for a row on Keuka Lake, N. Y., the other day and dangled her hand in the water over the edge of the boat. All at once she saw a lake trout dart toward her hand and she made a grab for it. She scooped the fish up into the boat, and it was found to be a trout weighing two pounds.

In Sumatra the wind decides the length of time a widow should remain single. Just after her husband's death she plants a flagstaff at her door, upon which a flag is raised. While the flag remains untorn by the wind, the etiquette of Sumatra forbids her to marry, but at the first rent, however tiny, she can lay aside her weeds, assume her most bewitching smile and accept the first man who presents himself.

A cat belonging to Sampson Alleman, of Tallyho, W. Va., killed a large copperhead snake the other day, after a vicious battle with the reptile. The cat was wandering around in the yard when it found the snake coiled up ready to spring. The cat sprang first and alighted on the back of the snake's neck. It bit viciously, but got away before the snake could strike. These tactics were repeated till the snake was worn out, when the cat bit it to death.

A student of Columbia University was living with his mother at one of the large hotels in New York. When preparing for an examination he often brought his books to the table and worked at Latin and Greek between the courses of his dinner. It happened one evening that he had considerable trouble over his Greek. The man who waited on the table saw his predicament and finally said quietly: "If you will let me come to you at such a time this evening I will be glad to help you over that translation." The boy was surprised, but eagerly reached for any aid in sight. It transpired that the waiter was a graduate of a European university, abundantly able to coach the puzzled student.

Nothing is more wonderful to investigators than the display of strength in insects compared with that in man. Ants will carry loads forty or fifty times as heavy as themselves. The beetle can move a weight one hundred and twelve times his own weight. The house-fly gives six hundred strokes of its wings in one second, and this enables it to go a distance of thirty-five feet. Probably the most wonderful of all is the dragon-fly. It can speed through the air at the rate of sixty miles an hour, and, more wonderful still, can stop instantaneously in its flight or move backward or sideways without changing the position of its body. Hundreds of bees can hang one to another without tearing away the feet of the upper one. It has been estimated that if an elephant were as strong in proportion to its weight as a male beetle it would be able to overturn a "skyscraper." In leaping great distances this strength is shown in another phase. If a horse could jump as far in proportion to its weight as a flea can to his, the horse would jump about two thousand miles.

## WITH THE FUNNY FELLOWS.

"Well, my little man," inquired a visitor pleasantly, "who are you?" "I'm the baby's brother," was the ingenuous reply.

Mistress—Bridget, it always seems to me that the crankiest mistresses get the best cooks. Cook—Ah! Go on wid yer blarney!

"Your horse isn't timid, I suppose?" "Timid? Why, my dear sir, he sleeps every night alone in his stable without any light."

Father—What makes you so extravagant with my money, sir? Son—Well, dad, I thought you wouldn't like to spend it yourself after working so hard for it.

Little Girl—I want a cake of soap. Chemist—Have it scented? Little Girl—No. I won't have it scented. I'll take it with me; we only live around the corner.

The Lady—I want a hat for my husband, please, but I've no idea what size he takes. The Shop Assistant—I should say about twelve and a half, madam. Gents who have their hats chosen by their wives usually take about that size.

In an outward-bound Boston car the other evening there was not a seat left. A woman entered and not a man noticed her standing, apparently. Finally one man rose from his seat and offered it to the woman. She thanked him, adding: "You are the only gentleman in the car." She was startled by the answer. "Yer betcher yer life I am, kiddo."

The druggist danced and chortled till the bottles danced on the shelves. "What's up?" asked the soda clerk, "have you been taking something?" "No," gurgled the dope dispenser ecstatically. "But do you remember when your water pipes were frozen last winter?" "Yes; but what—" "The plumber who fixed them has just brought a prescription to be filled."

Mrs. McGuire—Is your old man any better since he wint to th' doctor's, Mrs. Finegan? Mrs. Finegan—Not wan bit, Mrs. McGuire; it's worse th' poor man is wid his head whirlin' aroun' an' aroun,' tryin' to discover how to follow th' doctor's directions. Mrs. McGuire—An' what are th' directions, Mrs. Finegan? Mrs. Finegan—Sure, they do be to take wan powder six toimes a day, Mrs. McGuire.

A man went into the ticket office of the Colorado Midland Railway, at Seventeenth and California streets, recently, and said to Mr. Whitley, the ticket agent: "I want to get a ticket to Lame Water, Col." "To what place?" asked the perplexed ticket man. "Lame Water—It's a mining camp." Whitley put his head in his hands and thought deeply a moment. "Oh," he said finally, "you mean Cripple Creek, don't you?" "Yes, that's the place," said the man. "I got it wrong."

## These Books Tell You Everything!
## A COMPLETE SET IS A REGULAR ENCYCLOPEDIA!

Each book consists of sixty-four pages, printed on good paper, in clear type and neatly bound in an attractive, illustrated cover. Most of the books are also profusely illustrated, and all of the subjects treated upon are explained in such a simple manner that any child can thoroughly understand them. Look over the list as classified and see if you want to know anything about the subjects mentioned.

THESE BOOKS ARE FOR SALE BY ALL NEWSDEALERS OR WILL BE SENT BY MAIL TO ANY ADDRESS FROM THIS OFFICE ON RECEIPT OF PRICE, TEN CENTS EACH, OR ANY THREE BOOKS FOR TWENTY-FIVE CENTS. POSTAGE STAMPS TAKEN THE SAME AS MONEY. Address FRANK TOUSEY, Publisher, 24 Union Square, N.Y.

### MESMERISM

No. 81. HOW TO MESMERIZE.—Containing the most approved methods of mesmerism; also how to cure all kinds of diseases by animal magnetism, or, magnetic healing. By Prof. Leo Hugo Koch, A. C. S., author of "How to Hypnotize," etc.

### PALMISTRY.

No. 82. HOW TO DO PALMISTRY.—Containing the most approved methods of reading the lines on the hand, together with a full explanation of their meaning. Also explaining phrenology, and the key for telling character by the bumps on the head. By Leo Hugo Koch, A. C. S. Fully illustrated.

### HYPNOTISM.

43

No. 83. HOW TO HYPNOTIZE.—Containing valuable and instructive information regarding the science of hypnotism. Also explaining the most approved methods which are employed by the leading hypnotists of the world. By Leo Hugo Koch, A. C. S.

## SPORTING.

No. 21. HOW TO HUNT AND FISH.—The most complete hunting and fishing guide ever published. It contains full instructions about guns, hunting dogs, traps, trapping and fishing, together with descriptions of game and fish.

No. 26. HOW TO ROW, SAIL AND BUILD A BOAT.—Fully illustrated. Every boy should know how to row and sail a boat. Full instructions are given in this little book, together with instructions on swimming and riding, companion sports to boating.

No. 47. HOW TO BREAK, RIDE AND DRIVE A HORSE.—A complete treatise on the horse. Describing the most useful horses for business, the best horses for the road; also valuable recipes for diseases peculiar to the horse.

No. 48. HOW TO BUILD AND SAIL CANOES.—A handy book for boys, containing full directions for constructing canoes and the most popular manner of sailing them. Fully illustrated. By C. Stansfield Hicks.

## FORTUNE TELLING.

No. 1. NAPOLEON'S ORACULUM AND DREAM BOOK.—Containing the great oracle of human destiny; also the true meaning of almost any kind of dreams, together with charms, ceremonies, and curious games of cards. A complete book.

No. 23. HOW TO EXPLAIN DREAMS.—Everybody dreams, from the little child to the aged man and woman. This little book gives the explanation to all kinds of dreams, together with lucky and unlucky days, and "Napoleon's Oraculum," the book of fate.

No. 28. HOW TO TELL FORTUNES.—Everyone is desirous of knowing what his future life will bring forth, whether happiness or misery, wealth or poverty. You can tell by a glance at this little book. Buy one and be convinced. Tell your own fortune. Tell the fortune of your friends.

No. 76. HOW TO TELL FORTUNES BY THE HAND.—Containing rules for telling fortunes by the aid of lines of the hand, or the secret of palmistry. Also the secret of telling future events by aid of moles, marks, scars, etc. Illustrated. By A. Anderson.

## ATHLETIC.

No. 6. HOW TO BECOME AN ATHLETE.—Giving full instruction for the use of dumb bells, Indian clubs, parallel bars, horizontal bars and various other methods of developing a good healthy muscle; containing over sixty illustrations. Every boy can become strong and healthy by following the instructions contained in this little book.

No. 10. HOW TO BOX.—The art of self-defense made easy. Containing over thirty illustrations of guards, blows, and the different positions of a good boxer. Every boy should obtain one of these useful and instructive books, as it will teach you how to box without an instructor.

No. 25. HOW TO BECOME A GYMNAST.—Containing full instructions for all kinds of gymnastic sports and athletic exercises. Embracing thirty-five illustrations. By Professor W. Macdonald. A handy and useful book.

No. 34. HOW TO FENCE.—Containing full instruction for fencing and the use of the broadsword; also instruction in archery. Described with twenty-one practical illustrations, giving the best positions in fencing. A complete book.

## TRICKS WITH CARDS.

No. 51. HOW TO DO TRICKS WITH CARDS.—Containing explanations of the general principles of sleight-of-hand applicable to card tricks; of card tricks with ordinary cards, and not requiring sleight-of-hand; of tricks involving sleight-of-hand, or the use of specially prepared cards. By Professor Haffner. Illustrated.

No. 72. HOW TO DO SIXTY TRICKS WITH CARDS.—Embracing all of the latest and most deceptive card tricks, with illustrations. By A. Anderson.

No. 77. HOW TO DO FORTY TRICKS WITH CARDS.—Containing deceptive Card Tricks as performed by leading conjurors and magicians. Arranged for home amusement. Fully illustrated.

## MAGIC.

No. 2. HOW TO DO TRICKS.—The great book of magic and card tricks, containing full instruction on all the leading card tricks of the day, also the most popular magical illusions as performed by our leading magicians; every boy should obtain a copy of this book, as it will both amuse and instruct.

No. 22. HOW TO DO SECOND SIGHT.—Heller's second sight explained by his former assistant, Fred Hunt, Jr. Explaining how the secret dialogues were carried on between the magician and the boy on the stage; also giving all the codes and signals. The only authentic explanation of second sight.

No. 43. HOW TO BECOME A MAGICIAN.—Containing the grandest assortment of magical illusions ever placed before the public. Also tricks with cards, incantations, etc.

No. 68. HOW TO DO CHEMICAL TRICKS.—Containing over one hundred highly amusing and instructive tricks with chemicals. By A. Anderson. Handsomely illustrated.

No. 69. HOW TO DO SLEIGHT OF HAND.—Containing over fifty of the latest and best tricks used by magicians. Also containing the secret of second sight. Fully illustrated. By A. Anderson.

No. 70. HOW TO MAKE MAGIC TOYS.—Containing full directions for making Magic Toys and devices of many kinds. By A. Anderson. Fully illustrated.

No. 73. HOW TO DO TRICKS WITH NUMBERS.—Showing many curious tricks with figures and the magic of numbers. By A. Anderson. Fully illustrated.

No. 75. HOW TO BECOME A CONJUROR.—Containing tricks with Dominos, Dice, Cups and Balls, Hats, etc. Embracing thirty-six illustrations. By A. Anderson.

No. 78. HOW TO DO THE BLACK ART.—Containing a complete description of the mysteries of Magic and Sleight of Hand, together with many wonderful experiments. By A. Anderson. Illustrated.

## MECHANICAL.

No. 29. HOW TO BECOME AN INVENTOR.—Every boy should know how inventions originated. This book explains them all, giving examples in electricity, hydraulics, magnetism, optics, pneumatics, mechanics, etc. The most instructive book published.

No. 56. HOW TO BECOME AN ENGINEER.—Containing full instructions how to proceed in order to become a locomotive engineer; also directions for building a model locomotive: together with a full description of everything an engineer should know.

No. 57. HOW TO MAKE MUSICAL INSTRUMENTS—Full directions how to make a Banjo, Violin, Zither, Æolian Harp. Xylophone and other musical instrument; together with a brief description of nearly every musical instrument used in ancient or modern times. Profusely illustrated. By Algernon S. Fitzgerald, for twenty years bandmaster of the Royal Bengal Marines.

No. 59. HOW TO MAKE A MAGIC LANTERN.—Containing a description of the lantern, together with its history and invention. Also full directions for its use and for painting slides. Handsomely illustrated. By John Allen.

No. 71. HOW TO DO MECHANICAL TRICKS.—Containing complete instructions for performing over sixty Mechanical Tricks. By A. Anderson. Fully illustrated.

## LETTER WRITING.

No. 11. HOW TO WRITE LOVE-LETTERS—A most complete little book, containing full directions for writing love-letters, and when to use them, giving specimen letters for young end old.

No. 12. HOW TO WRITE LETTERS TO LADIES.—Giving complete instructions for writing letters to ladies on all subjects; also letters of introduction, notes and requests.

No. 24. HOW TO WRITE LETTERS TO GENTLEMEN.—Containing full directions for writing to gentlemen on all subjects; also giving sample letters for instruction.

No. 53. HOW TO WRITE LETTERS.—A wonderful little book, telling you how to write to your sweetheart, your father, mother, sister, brother, employer; and, in fact, everybody and anybody you wish to write to. Every young man and every young lady in the land should have this book.

45

No. 74. HOW TO WRITE LETTERS CORRECTLY.—Containing full instructions for writing letters on almost any subject; also rules for punctuation and composition, with specimen letters.

## THE STAGE.

No. 41. THE BOYS OF NEW YORK END MEN'S JOKE BOOK.—Containing a great variety of the latest jokes used by the most famous end men. No amateur minstrels is complete without this wonderful little book.

No. 42. THE BOYS OF NEW YORK STUMP SPEAKER.—Containing a varied assortment of stump speeches, Negro, Dutch and Irish. Also end men's jokes. Just the thing for home amusement and amateur shows.

No. 45. THE BOYS OF NEW YORK MINSTREL GUIDE AND JOKE BOOK.—Something new and very instructive. Every boy should obtain this book, as it contains full instructions for organizing an amateur minstrel troupe.

No. 65. MULDOON'S JOKES.—This is one of the most original joke books ever published, and it is brimful of wit and humor. It contains a large collection of songs, jokes, conundrums, etc., of Terrence Muldoon, the great wit, humorist, and practical joker of the day. Every boy who can enjoy a good substantial joke should obtain a copy immediately.

No. 79. HOW TO BECOME AN ACTOR.—Containing complete instructions how to make up for various characters on the stage; together with the duties of the Stage Manager, Prompter, Scenic Artist and Property Man. By a prominent Stage Manager.

No. 80. GUS WILLIAMS' JOKE BOOK.—Containing the latest jokes, anecdotes and funny stories of this world-renowned and ever popular German comedian. Sixty-four pages; handsome colored cover containing a half-tone photo of the author.

## HOUSEKEEPING.

No. 16. HOW TO KEEP A WINDOW GARDEN.—Containing full instructions for constructing a window garden either in town or country, and the most approved methods for raising beautiful flowers at home. The most complete book of the kind ever published.

No. 30. HOW TO COOK.—One of the most instructive books on cooking ever published. It contains recipes for cooking meats, fish, game, and oysters; also pies, puddings, cakes and all kinds of pastry, and a grand collection of recipes by one of our most popular cooks.

No. 37. HOW TO KEEP HOUSE.—It contains information for everybody, boys, girls, men and women; it will teach you how to make almost anything around the house, such as parlor ornaments, brackets, cements, Æolian harps, and bird lime for catching birds.

## ELECTRICAL.

No. 46. HOW TO MAKE AND USE ELECTRICITY.—A description of the wonderful uses of electricity and electro magnetism; together with full instructions for making Electric Toys, Batteries, etc. By George Trebel, A. M., M. D. Containing over fifty illustrations.

No. 64. HOW TO MAKE ELECTRICAL MACHINES.—Containing full directions for making electrical machines, induction coils, dynamos, and many novel toys to be worked by electricity. By R. A. R. Bennett. Fully illustrated.

No. 67. HOW TO DO ELECTRICAL TRICKS.—Containing a large collection of instructive and highly amusing electrical tricks, together with illustrations. By A. Anderson.

## ENTERTAINMENT.

No. 9. HOW TO BECOME A VENTRILOQUIST.—By Harry Kennedy. The secret given away. Every intelligent boy reading this book of instructions, by a practical professor (delighting multitudes every night with his wonderful imitations), can master the art, and create any amount of fun for himself and friends. It is the greatest book ever published, and there's millions (of fun) in it.

No. 20. HOW TO ENTERTAIN AN EVENING PARTY.—A very valuable little book just published. A complete compendium of games, sports, card diversions, comic recitations, etc. suitable for parlor or drawing room entertainment. It contains more for the money than any book published.

No. 35. HOW TO PLAY GAMES.—A complete and useful little book, containing the rules and regulations of billiards, bagatelle, backgammon, croquet, dominoes, etc.

No. 36. HOW TO SOLVE CONUNDRUMS—Containing all the leading conundrums of the day, amusing riddles, curious catches and witty sayings.

No. 52. HOW TO PLAY CARDS.—A complete and handy little book, giving the rules and full directions for playing Euchre, Cribbage, Casino, Forty-Five, Rounce, Pedro Sancho, Draw Poker, Auction Pitch, All Fours, and many other popular games of cards.

No. 66. HOW TO DO PUZZLES.—Containing over three hundred interesting puzzles and conundrums, with key to same. A complete book. Fully illustrated. By A. Anderson.

## ETIQUETTE.

No. 13. HOW TO DO IT; OR, BOOK OF ETIQUETTE.—It is a great life secret, and one that every young man desires to know all about. There's happiness in it.

No. 33. HOW TO BEHAVE.—Containing the rules and etiquette of good society and the easiest and most approved methods of appearing to good advantage at parties, balls, the theatre, church, and in the drawing-room.

## DECLAMATION.

No. 27. HOW TO RECITE AND BOOK OF RECITATIONS.—Containing the most popular selections in use, comprising Dutch dialect, French dialect, Yankee and Irish dialect pieces, together with many standard readings.

No. 31. HOW TO BECOME A SPEAKER.—Containing fourteen illustrations, giving the different positions requisite to become a good speaker, reader and elocutionist. Also containing gems from all the popular authors of prose and poetry, arranged in the most simple and concise manner possible.

No. 49. HOW TO DEBATE.—Giving rules for conducting debates, outlines for debates, questions for discussion, and the best sources for procuring information on the questions given.

## SOCIETY.

No. 3. HOW TO FLIRT.—The arts and wiles of flirtation are fully explained by this little book. Besides the various methods of handkerchief, fan, glove, parasol, window and hat flirtation, it contains a full list of the language and sentiment of flowers, which is interesting to everybody, both old and young. You cannot be happy without one.

No. 4. HOW TO DANCE.—Is the title of a new and handsome little book just issued by Frank Tousey. It contains full instructions in the art of dancing, etiquette in the ball-room and at parties, how to dress, and full directions for calling off in all popular square dances.

No. 5. HOW TO MAKE LOVE.—A complete guide to love, courtship and marriage, giving sensible advice, rules and etiquette to be observed, with many curious and interesting things not generally known.

No. 17. HOW TO DRESS.—Containing full instruction in the art of dressing and appearing well at home and abroad, giving the selections of colors, material, and how to have them made up.

No. 18. HOW TO BECOME BEAUTIFUL.—One of the brightest and most valuable little books ever given to the world. Everybody wishes to know how to become beautiful, both male and female. The secret is simple, and almost costless. Read this book and be convinced how to become beautiful.

## BIRDS AND ANIMALS.

No. 7. HOW TO KEEP BIRDS.—Handsomely illustrated and containing full instructions for the management and training of the canary, mockingbird, bobolink, blackbird, paroquet, parrot, etc.

No. 30. HOW TO RAISE DOGS, POULTRY, PIGEONS AND RABBITS.—A useful and instructive book. Handsomely illustrated. By Ira Drofraw.

No. 40. HOW TO MAKE AND SET TRAPS.—Including hints on how to catch moles, weasels, otter, rats, squirrels and birds. Also how to cure skins. Copiously illustrated. By J. Harrington Keene.

No. 50. HOW TO STUFF BIRDS AND ANIMALS.—A valuable book, giving instructions in collecting, preparing, mounting and preserving birds, animals and insects.

No. 54. HOW TO KEEP AND MANAGE PETS.—Giving complete information as to the manner and method of raising, keeping, taming, breeding, and managing all kinds of pets; also giving full instructions for making cages, etc. Fully explained by twenty-eight illustrations, making it the most complete book of the kind ever published.

## MISCELLANEOUS.

No. 8. HOW TO BECOME A SCIENTIST.—A useful and instructive book, giving a complete treatise on chemistry, also experiments in acoustics, mechanics, mathematics, chemistry, and directions for making fireworks, colored fires, and gas balloons. This book cannot be equaled.

No. 14. HOW TO MAKE CANDY.—A complete hand-book for making all kinds of candy, ice-cream, syrups, essences, etc., etc.

No. 34. HOW TO BECOME AN AUTHOR.—Containing full information regarding choice of subjects, the use of words and the manner of preparing and submitting manuscript. Also containing valuable information as to the neatness, legibility and general composition of manuscript, essential to a successful author. By Prince Hiland.

No. 38. HOW TO BECOME YOUR OWN DOCTOR.—A wonderful book, containing useful and practical information in the treatment of ordinary diseases and ailments common to every family. Abounding in useful and effective recipes for general complaints.

No. 55. HOW TO COLLECT STAMPS AND COINS.—Containing valuable information regarding the collecting and arranging of stamps and coins. Handsomely illustrated.

No. 58. HOW TO BE A DETECTIVE.—By Old King Brady, the world-known detective. In which he lays down some valuable and sensible rules for beginners, and also relates some adventures and experiences of well-known detectives.

No. 60. HOW TO BECOME A PHOTOGRAPHER.—Containing useful information regarding the Camera and how to work it; also how to make Photographic Magic Lantern Slides and other Transparencies. Handsomely illustrated. By Captain W. De W. Abney.

No. 62. HOW TO BECOME A WEST POINT MILITARY CADET.—Containing full explanations how to gain admittance, course of Study, Examinations, Duties, Staff of Officers, Post Guard, Police Regulations, Fire Department, and all a boy should know to be a Cadet. Compiled and written by Lu Senarens, author of "How to Become a Naval Cadet."

No. 63. HOW TO BECOME A NAVAL CADET.—Complete instructions of how to gain admission to the Annapolis Naval Academy. Also containing the course of instruction, description of grounds and buildings, historical sketch, and everything a boy should know to become an officer in the United States Navy. Compiled and written by Lu Senarens, author of "How to Become a West Point Military Cadet."

PRICE 10 CENTS EACH, OR 3 FOR 25 CENTS.
Address FRANK TOUSEY, Publisher, 24 Union Square, New York.

### Latest Issues

### "All Around Weekly"
Containing Stories of All Kinds.
COLORED COVERS. 32 PAGES. PRICE 5 CENTS.
36 Iceberg Jack, the Hero of the Arctic.37 The Island Captive; or, Donald Kane's Victory.38 Saved in Time; or, The Downward Course of Dick Ballard.39 The Black Cross; or, The Mysteries of the Jungle.40 The Boy Wizard of the Nile; or, The Mystery of Pharaoh's Temple.41 Deserted in Dismal Swamp; or, The Secrets of the Lone Hut.42 Danger Signal Dave, the Daring Boy Engineer of the West.43 Matt the Avenger; or, Fighting the Mexican Bandits.

## "Wild West Weekly"
A Magazine Containing Stories, Sketches, Etc., of Western Life.
COLORED COVERS. 32 PAGES. PRICE 5 CENTS.

403 Young Wild West's Shower of Gold; or, Arietta's Lucky Slip.404 Young Wild West as a Scout; or, Saving the Emigrant Train.405 Young Wild West Running the Ranch; or, Arietta's Game Fight.406 Young Wild West and "Chapparal Chick"; or, The Bandits of the Foothills.407 Young Wild West and the Mad Mexican; or, Arietta's Warning Shot.408 Young Wild West and the Cowboy Millionaire; or, Hemmed in by Enemies.409 Young Wild West in the "Land of Dead Things"; or, Arietta and the Vultures.

## "The Liberty Boys of '76"
A Magazine Containing Stories of the American Revolution.
COLORED COVERS. 32 PAGES. PRICE 5 CENTS.

499 The Liberty Boys' Pitched Battle; or, The Escape of the Indian Spy.500 The Liberty Boys' Light Artillery; or, Good Work at the Guns.501 The Liberty Boys and "Whistling Will"; or, The Mad Spy of Paulus Hook.502 The Liberty Boys' Underground Camp; or, In Strange Quarters.503 The Liberty Boys' Dandy Spy; or, Deceiving the Governor.

## "Fame and Fortune Weekly"
Containing Stories of Boys Who Make Money.
COLORED COVERS. 32 PAGES. PRICE 5 CENTS.

249 Learning a Trade; or, On the Road to Fortune.250 Buying on Margin; or, The Lad Who Won the Money. (A Wall Street story.)251 Joe Darcy's Treasure Hunt; or, The Secret of the Island Cave.252 A "Live" Boy; or, Quick to get the Dollars. (A story of Wall Street.)253 A Barrel of Coin; or, The Luck of a Boy Trader.254 Driven to the Wall; or, The Nerve of a Wall Street Boy.255 Johnny, the Parcel Boy; or, The Lad Who Saved the Firm.

## "Pluck and Luck"
Containing Stories of Adventure.
COLORED COVERS. 32 PAGES. PRICE 5 CENTS.

631 Cal the Canvas Boy; or, Two Years with a Circus. By men.632 Buffalo Bill's Boy Chum; or, In the Wild West with the King of Scouts. By an Old Scout.633 Bonnie Prince Hal; or, The Pride of the A. C. I. By Richard R. Montgomery.634 On Hand; or, The Boy Who was Always Ready. By Howard Austin.635 Arnold's Shadow; or, The Traitor's Nemesis. (A story of the American Revolution.) By Gen. Jas. A. Gordon.636 Adrift in the Tree Tops; or, The Fate of Two Boy Castaways. By Allyn Draper.637 Mustang Matt, the Prince of Cowboys. By An Old Scout.

## "Work and Win"
Containing the Great Fred Fearnot Stories.
COLORED COVERS. 32 PAGES. PRICE 5 CENTS.

607 Fred Fearnot at the Plate; or, The Game That Had to be Won.608 Fred Fearnot's War on Drink; or, Reforming a Hard Crowd.609 Fred Fearnot's Twenty-Inning Game; or, Winning Out at Last.610 Fred Fearnot's Search for Smith; or, The Man Who Could Not Be Found.611 Fred Fearnot at the Fair; or, Shaking Things Up at Shagtown.

For sale by all newsdealers, or will be sent to any address on receipt of price, 5 cents per copy, in money or postage stamps, by

FRANK TOUSEY, Publisher, 24 Union Square, New York.

## SECRET SERVICE
## OLD AND YOUNG KING BRADY, DETECTIVES.
Price 5 cents. 32 Pages. Colored Covers. Issued Weekly.
LATEST ISSUES:

527 The Bradys and the Fatal Despatch; or, The Mystery of Five Words.528 The Bradys Tracking a Stolen Ruby; or, After a Gang of Thieves.529 The Bradys and the Boy Shadower; or, A Very Hard Case to Solve.530 The Bradys Cunning Plot; or, Trapping the River Pirates.531 The Bradys and the Quong Lee; or, The Dog-faced Man of Chinatown.532 The Bradys and the Broken Handcuff; or, The Hunchback of the Old Red House.533 The Bradys Working for a Life; or, Exposing a Great Fraud.534 The Bradys and the Newsboy; or, Saved from the State Prison.535 The Bradys After the Beggars and Beats; or, The King of Misery Hall.536 The Bradys and the Poisoned Ring; or, Trailing a Shadow Gang.537 The Bradys at Deadman's Curve; or, Solving a Mystery of Union Square.538 The Bradys and the Pawn Ticket; or, The Old Maniac's Secret.539 The Bradys Trailing a Chinese Giant; or, The "Strong Arm" Men of Mott Street.540 The Bradys and the King of Rogues; or, Working Up the Dalton Case.541 The Bradys Top Floor Clew; or, The Mystery of a Tenement House.542 The Bradys and the Broken Clock; or, The Secret of Ten Minutes to Ten.543 The Bradys Fighting the Gold Coiners; or, On the Trail of the Black Hand.544 The Bradys and the Old Miser; or, The Secret of the Blue Room.545 The Bradys and the Diamond Dagger; or, The Mystery of a Missing Girl.546 The Bradys Shadowing a Chinaman; or, Trapping a Yellow Fiend.547 The Bradys and the Fatal Letter; or, The Messenger Boy's Secret.548 The Bradys After the Bridge Rushers; or, Rounding Up the Pick-pockets.549 The Bradys and the Forged Order; or, The Clew Found in the Cellar.550 The Bradys and the Reporter; or, Working Up a Newspaper Case.551 The Bradys Yellow Shadow; or, The Search for a Missing Gold King.552 The Bradys and the Skeleton Hand; or, The Strangest of All Clews.553 The Bradys Hidden Diamonds; or, The Great John Street Jewel Robbery.554 The Bradys at Hangman's Roost; or, The Mystery of the House on the Rocks.555 The Bradys and the Death Bell; or, The Secret of the Indian Juggler.556 The Bradys in the Doyers Street Den; or, A Curious Chinese Case.557 The Bradys and the "Black Boys"; or, The Fate of the Six Masks.558 The Bradys After the Bomb Throwers; or, Smashing the Anarchist League.559 The Bradys and the Man-Trappers; or, The Trail of the "Seven Sevens."560 The Bradys and "Joss House Jim"; or, Tracking a Chinese Crook.561 The Bradys Fatal Night; or, The Mystery of the Mad Sheriff.562 The Bradys and the Idol's Eye; or, The Clew of the Crystal Cross.563 The Bradys Chasing the Red League; or, Rounding up a Bowery Bunch.564 The Bradys and the Belt of Gold; or, Lost on the Great White Way.565 The Bradys after the Tong Kings; or, The Red Lady of Chinatown.566 The Bradys' Boston Doubles; or, Trapping the Fake Detectives.567 The Bradys' Bank Book Mystery; or, The Secret of the Torn Page.568 The Bradys and the Golden Comet; or, The Case of the Chinese Prince.569 The Bradys' Floating Clew; or, Solving a Morgue Mystery.570 The Bradys and "Brooklyn Bob"; or, The Boldest Crook in the World.571 The Bradys and the Bootblack; or, Bagging the "Boss of the Bead."572 The Bradys and the Blotted Check; or, Saved by the Scratch of a Pen.573 The Bradys and the Missing Witness; or, The Secret of the Hole in the Wall.574 The Bradys in Little China; or, The Mystery of a Mission House.575 The Bradys and the Midnight Men; or, A Fight for Five Lives.576 The Bradys' Fast Freight Mystery; or, The Case of Conductor King.577 The Bradys and the Six Gold Dollars; or, A Very Singular Clew.578 The Bradys and the Poisoned Arrow; or, The Mystery of Central Park.579 The Bradys and the Green Goods Men; or, The Shrewdest of Them All.580 The Bradys and Captain Crossbones; or, Bagging the Boss of the River Thieves.581 The Bradys and the Escaped Convict; or, The Clew That Came From States' Prison.582 The Bradys and the Ruby Locket; or, Solving a Society Mystery.583 The Bradys and "Red Light Dick;" or, After the Slum King.584 The Bradys Under a Cloud; or, Working for a Poor Boy.585 The Bradys and the Actor's Son; or, Sold into Slavery.586 The Bradys Tempted; or, Dealing Out

Justice.587 The Bradys and the Hidden Assassin; or, Winning in Record Time.588 The Bradys' Dark Work; or, The Mystery of a Night.589 The Bradys and the Mystic Band; or, Trailing the Silent Seven.590 The Bradys Drugged; or, Caught by the Chinese Crooks.591 The Bradys and the Black Snake Bracelet; or, Trapping a Society Queen.592 The Bradys After a "Lifer"; or, The Man Who Broke from Sing Sing.593 The Bradys and the Red Wolves; or, Working on the Great Brandon Case.594 The Bradys Box 2; or, Hunting Down a Tough Gang.595 The Bradys Telephone Mystery; or, The Clew that Came Over the Wires.596 The Bradys and the Marble Statue; or, Three Days of Mystery.597 The Bradys and the Bird of Prey; or, Shadowing the Crooks of Gotham.598 The Bradys Anarchists' Case; or, After the Bomb Throwers.599 The Bradys and the Cipher Message; or, Traced by a Telegram.600 The Bradys on the Saturday Special; or, Betrayed by a Baggage Check.601 The Bradys and the Hidden Man; or, The Haunted House on the Hill.602 The Bradys in the Toils; or, The Mystery of the Pretty Milliner.603 The Bradys and the Yellow Jar; or, The Great Percy Poisoning Case.604 The Bradys' Chinese Clew; or, The Secret Dens of Pell Street.

CPSIA information can be obtained at www.ICGtesting.com
Printed in the USA
BVOW04s0830231214

380563BV00028B/403/P